The Embittered of

OZ

By

Will Savive

Del-Grande Publishing

Hackensack, New Jersey
Copyright © 2022 Will Savive/Del-Grande
Publishing

ISBN: 978-1-7374865-6-5

Author's Website:

willsavive.com

The Embittered of

OZ

To get all the latest news on horror movies & books, join:

https://www.facebook.com/WillSavive

ISBN-13: 978-1-7374865-6-5
BISAC: Horror/Action-Adventure

Printed in the United States of America

Chapter 1 – Home for the Holidays

December 20th

It's 10:00 a.m. at *Newark International Airport* in Newark, NJ. A plane arriving from California has just landed. *Suzanne Millington* steps off the plane holding a carry-on duffle bag and purse. Suzanne is an attractive, classy brunette with an athletic figure, although it is hard to tell as she is bundled up in her winter clothing. She heads to the baggage area to retrieve her suitcase.

She texts her mother and gives her a status update. The airport is packed with holiday travelers. Most are wearing masks even though the Covid-19 mask mandate has been lifted. New variants continue to emerge, and many people still feel safer wearing a mask. Others are happy that they are not required to do so. Suzanne wore her mask on the plane but removed it after entering the terminal.

After retrieving her suitcase from the baggage carousel, Suzanne exits the airport and hops into a cab. She takes the very familiar drive down the New Jersey Turnpike. It's a short drive, about a half-hour, to her childhood home in Teaneck, NJ. She puts her wireless headphones in her ears and connects it to her phone via Bluetooth. She uses the *Amazon Music App* to choose from her long list of songs. She selects the song '*Let 'Em Cry*' from the new album by the *Red Hot Chilli Peppers, Unlimited Love*. She zones out while looking out the window and viewing the swamps and factories of NJ on her way home. She can't help but recall her many trips with friends to the Jersey shore as she looks out onto the familiar scenery.

Her phone rings as she nears her childhood home.

"Hi, mom," Suzanne says.

"Are you almost home?" her mother asks.

"I'm like," Suzanne looks at the GPS in the cab stuck to the middle vent of the dashboard, "three minutes away."

"Ok, I will send your brother out to help you with your bags."

Her brother is outside awaiting her arrival as she pulls up. The driver pops the trunk as Suzanne exits the cab.

"Hey, screensaver!" Suzanne says as she hugs him.

"Really, you are still calling me that?" he replies as he hugs her.

"Well, last time I saw you, you did nothing all day but sleep!" she insinuates.

"Yeah, well, I have a job now and a girlfriend," he sneers. "And she's here, so be nice!"

"You have a girlfriend?" she replies sarcastically. "Let the games begin!"

"That's not funny, Suzy!" he blurts

anxiously. "She knows me as Will. Please don't embarrass me!"

"Will?" she asks, puzzled. "You are Billy!"

"Not anymore!" he states adamantly. "I'm older now. 'Will' suits me better. Plus, my name is William. I have no clue why the hell I've been called Billy all my life!"

"I can't wait to tell her how you pissed the bed till you were fifteen!"

"I swear, I will friggen kill you! I'm not playing, Suzanne!" he responds.

"How's Dad?" she asks.

"You know, he is in remission but still not out of the woods just yet. Mom is taking good care of him, though, as always." Will grabs her duffle bag and then her large suitcase from the trunk. He is a lean, muscular, good-looking eighteen-year-old senior in high school.

"Jesus!" he says as he struggles to remove her bag from the trunk. "How the hell long are you planning on staying?"

"A woman needs her stuff! You wouldn't know the first thing, wallpaper!"

"You are gonna get it this weekend, I swear!" Will says impatiently. "This ain't

2015. I'm a grown man now!" Will walks up to her spitefully. "I'm the man of the house now!"

"Oh, so you are the man now?" Suzanne asks facetiously. She chuckles. "Whenever I arrive, you are immediately second in command, and you know this! And don't try and challenge me either, cause you know what will happen!"

"Ok, ok; I'm just kidding, jeez!" he responds submissively. "You still can't take a joke," he scoffs.

"Mom!" Suzanne shouts as she sees her mother, *Sarah*, standing in the doorway. Suzanne rushes and hugs her tightly.

"My baby!" her mother says while squeezing her.

Family Time

Suzanne's mother has a feast prepared for her four children. Everyone appreciates her home cooking. They all finally take their seats in the dining room. Suzanne's mother, Sarah, sits at the head of the table with her back to the window. Her father, *Joel*, sits at the head of the table on the opposite side. His back is facing the living room. *Suzanne* [22] is seated on the left side of the table closest to her mother. *Beverly* [17] is sitting to the right of Suzanne. *Christopher* [15] is sitting opposite Suzanne. Finally, *Adam* [18] is seated across from Beverly, closest to his father, and his girlfriend, *Amanda*, sits between him and his brother.

Usually, all of the food is placed on the table and passed around. However, this year Suzanne's mother decided to break tradition and do it buffet style. Three long tables, covered with matching Christmas tablecloths, lay side by side, resting against the wall behind Adam and Christopher. Several heated buffet trays line the tables. Everyone has filled their plates for round one.

"Time to say grace," Sarah announces. "Who would like to do the honors, Suzanne?"

"I think it should be, dad!" Adam suggests. No one objects. Everyone closes their eyes and holds hands around the table.

"Dear Lord, thank you for blessing us with this special family dinner," Joel proclaims. "Please bless this food and watch over us on what is likely my last Christmas dinner with my family."

"You couldn't help yourself, could you, dad?" Adam says.

"What?" Joel says. "I am just being real. You know, keeping it real, like you kids say!"

"Let's keep it festive, dad," Suzanne responds. He reluctantly nods in agreement.

"Good food, good meat, good God, let's eat!" Joel voices. With that, everyone begins digging in.

"Oh my God, mom, this is so good!" Beverly declares.

"Yeah, mom, you have outdone yourself," Adam says.

"Thank you!" Sarah mentions humbly. "It took me a little more time this year, but I got it done."

"So, Suzanne, how is my alma mater treating you?" her father asks.

"School is great, dad," Suzanne responds. "UCLA was such a great choice!"

"Have you figured out your major yet?" her father asks.

"I am majoring in criminal justice," Suzanne responds.

"As long as it's not public speaking," Adam replies. "Remember the time you tried to speak publicly at the school play?" Adam turns to Amanda and speaks softly, "She had one line, froze up, and ran off the stage!" he and Christopher giggle in amusement.

"Leave your sister alone," Sarah commands. "She has always had stage fright, even as a little girl. She gets anxiety speaking in front of crowds," Sarah explains to Amanda.

"Thanks for the words of encouragement, mom," Suzanne says facetiously. Suzanne turns her attention to Adam. "Amanda, did Adam tell you that he used to piss the bed in his sleep until he was sixteen?" Suzanne asks. Adam looks at Amanda.

"That's not true!" Adam says adamantly.

"You are gonna lie to your girlfriend with a straight face?" Suzanne asks.

Amanda looks at Adam with a confused look.

"Ok, ok, let's keep it civil, you two," Sarah says firmly.

"Mom, since we are keeping it real," Suzanne says, "am I telling the truth?"

"Adam had a bladder issue, it's true," their mother confirms. "But he is over it now."

"Really, mom?" Adam barks. "Thanks a lot!" He is embarrassed. Suzanne looks at Amanda and laughs. Amanda almost spits out her drink from laughing so hard. This annoys Adam even more. He leans over to Suzanne and whispers in her ear, "Ok, you win! Cut it out!"

Once Suzanne finished the food on her plate, she asked to be excused, saying she needed to make a phone call. Suzanne walks out toward the sliding glass doors that lead to the backyard. She stops and looks around cautiously to see if anyone is following her before opening the doors. Then, she quietly enters the backyard, making sure to do so silently. She walks around to the side of the house and pulls out a pack of cigarettes from her purse. She searches her bag frantically for a lighter but cannot find one.

"Shit!" she whispers. Just then, Christopher walks around the corner of the house with a lit cigarette in his mouth. When he sees Suzanne, he is in shock. He freezes.

"Oh, damn!" he babbles.

"You are smoking cigarettes now?" Suzanne says in disapproval.

"You smoke too," he responds.

"I'm of age!" she replies.

"I used to see you sneak out here to smoke when you were in high school," Christopher explains.

"You did?" Suzanne asks. "You little stalker! Give me a light." Christopher hands Suzanne his lighter. Suzanne lights her cigarette and puts the lighter in the front pocket of her jeans.

"Please don't tell mom and dad I am smoking!" Christopher asks.

"I won't tell if you don't tell," Suzanne replies. Their parents have no idea either one of them smokes.

After a long weekend with her family, Suzanne has her suitcase and duffle bag packed. She is ready for the ride to the airport and the long flight back to California. After saying her heart-felt goodbyes, she heads to the airport and boards her plane. She couldn't wait to return to UCLA to see her friends and enjoy her freedom. However, she did not know that her journey back to California was about to take a lot longer than expected!

Easy Victor

Suzanne buckles her seatbelt at the request of the captain via microphone. Minutes later, the plane begins to taxi onto the runway. The plane pauses for a moment as it is lined up on the runway, awaiting the tower's order to take off. Once the order is given, the plane accelerates down the runway. The sounds and vibrations increase as the plane quickly picks up speed. The engines go from a gentle purr to a giant roar. Within seconds, the force pushes all passengers back into their seats. Suzanne experiences a lurch in her stomach as the plane lifts off the runway.

Suzanne sits back in her seat and

closes her eyes. Several passengers get tunnel vision, and their muscles tense up as the plane rises. Many passengers start breathing heavily, bracing themselves as the plane's wheels retract and the nose quickly ascends. However, Suzanne has a special technique that she has developed to keep her calm during takeoff. She relaxes her muscles, lightens herself, and has a planned distraction for her mind to obviate thinking about the stressful event taking place. Moreover, she simply doesn't have any fear of flying, nor does she find it dangerous. In fact, she finds driving much more dangerous and stressful.

The ground quickly falls away, and the once massive terminal building soon looks like Lego pieces. As the plane climbs, it experiences *wake turbulence*, in which a disturbance in the atmosphere forms behind the aircraft as it passes through the air. The plane shakes. The passengers feel like they are driving on an extremely bumpy road. Soon, the unrest halts, the engines throttle back slightly, and the plane's angle lowers as it settles into a climb. Everyone takes a collective breath as the plane levels off and stabilizes.

"I didn't think we were going to make it there for a second," the red-headed female sitting to the right of Suzanne says to her.

"Is this your first time flying?" Suzanne asks.

"Yeah, how'd you know?"

"Cause this is pretty typical of any flight takeoff," Suzanne responds.

"Oh, that's good to know!" the woman says. "I was so nervous getting on this plane. I had an awful dream about this trip last night."

"It's first-time jitters," Suzanne replies. "We've all had them! Just try and relax. We will be there in no time."

"Thank you for the comforting words," the woman says.

Suzanne rests her head against the seat's headrest. She closes her eyes and hits play on her phone. Her wireless headphones begin playing the song *"Bring Me to Life"* by *Evanescence*. Suzanne is so relaxed that she dozes off for a few moments.

Suddenly she is jolted in her seat and

thrown forward aggressively into her seatbelt. She opens her eyes to frightened screams from several passengers. Suzanne's heart starts racing when she sees the commotion. She begins taking shallow, gasping breaths as she looks around at the faces of panicking passengers. The plane is violently vacillating from side to side unnaturally. The song *"Say it Ain't So"* by *Weezer* is playing. She quickly pulls out her headphones and hears a chorus of terrifying and unnerving screams. Suzanne looks at the seat to her right—where the red-headed female was sitting earlier—and sees it is empty.

"Ladies and gentlemen!" the captain says shakily over the loudspeaker. "We are experiencing extreme turbulence! Please buckle your seatbelts and put your head between your legs." Suzanne exhales raggedly as she is thrown around her seat. Moments later, she hears the pilot say *"Easy Victor,"* in a desperate voice over the intercom. As the plane shook uncontrollably, the red-headed woman who was seated next to Suzanne earlier had the misfortune of being in the bathroom. She is tossed around the small lavatory like clothes in a washing machine. She soon loses consciousness.

The lights in the cabin begin to flicker before complete darkness ensues. Each passenger experiences a sinking feeling in their stomach. Much like a free fall, a sense of weightlessness overcomes them. In total darkness, the terrifying, nightmarish screams are maddening. Suzanne remains calm and starts praying as her body jounces to and fro.

BANG!

The giant plane crashes down with the sounds of several metallic thuds and metallic scrapings. The plane splits into several pieces, and the sounds of blood-curdling screams immediately halt and shift to a disturbing silence.

Chapter 2 – Welcome to Oz

Where Am I?

There is a faint sound of static crackling amidst the silence and darkness. There is also a low electronic humming sound and intermittent metallic creeks. Suzanne coughs loudly and then opens her eyes.

'What the hell just happened?' her inner voice asks her. For a moment, she thinks she is home in her bed. However, she feels intense pain in her back and head when she starts to sit up. She whimpers, and feels groggy. She doesn't recall being in a plane crash. Soon, all of her senses start coming back, all at once. It's overwhelming. First, she hears the numerous mechanical sounds. Although faint, they are deafening to her amidst the silence and bewilderment. Next, she smells the strange odors of things burning, like metal mixed with human flesh. It is nothing like she has ever smelt before and indeed not pleasant. Her eyes slowly begin adjusting to the darkness. Looking around, she remembers her last thoughts before blacking out.

Fragmented flashes of the terrifying moments just before impact dance in her head. 'Oh, my God,' she thinks. 'I was just in a plane crash!' She goes from calm to overanxious and terrified in a moment. 'Am I dead?' she wonders. Her adrenaline spikes furiously. She gets to her feet, forgetting about the pain, and looks around. Her eyes are gradually adjusting to the darkness. Ahead, she sees a flickering electronic light from an exposed wire hanging from overhead that is still active. She also sees a dim light ahead, which looks like an overhead light above a seat.

"Hello?" she shouts. No one answers. "Hello? Is anyone here?" Still, she hears no one. She starts to think that maybe she had been accidentally left behind.

She takes a step toward the lights but stumbles over something. She reaches into her pocket for her cell phone. She takes it out, turns on the flashlight, and shines it toward her feet. She lets out a horrific scream! "Oh, my God, no!" She had stumbled over a hand covered in blood. She shifts the light to get a glimpse at more of the person's body. It's a man. There is a crack in his head that is oozing blood. He is clearly dead. She becomes frantic. She vacillates her cell phone light in all directions. She sees dead body after dead body, and all the gruesome details of their deaths are on display.

She moves forward, looking for an exit. Dead bodies are everywhere! She locates an emergency exit. She puts her phone in her pocket and grabs the handle. She pushes the handle down and pushes outward, but it doesn't budge. She pushes it up and pushes outward, but it still doesn't budge. Feeling trapped, her level of panic increases dramatically. She grabs the handle and starts shaking it hysterically. "Come on!" she shouts. She throws her shoulder into the door a few times. Suddenly, she is hit by something that knocks her to the ground, and she feels a weight resting on her left hip. She turns to her left and sees a dead female's eyes looking right at her. She sees the blood dripping off of the female's head and onto her face. She screams in fear, grimaces, then pushes the body off her in disgust. She gets to her feet and riotously begins searching for another exit. So hysterical is she that she ignores the bodies she is stepping on along the way.

She finds another emergency exit. Again, she tries to open it, but this one is also jammed. She pushes harder and harder this time, as she begins weeping furiously. All of the emotions are now starting to hit her. She believes she is going to die in this wreck. "Help! Help!" she screams as she continues to ram her right shoulder into the door. After numerous tries, it opens swiftly.

Clang!

The force of her thrust sends her falling out of the plane. She falls about three feet before belly-flopping onto the grass. She winces and whimpers as she raises her head slowly, then gasps and groans. Her pain again takes a back seat as she gazes upon the mysterious land. A plethora of bright colors overwhelms her senses. The aesthetic beauty is palpable. She slowly raises to her feet in awe. Looking outward, she sees tall trees bearing succulent fruits, well-landscaped grass that looks almost like turf because of how well-kept it is, beautiful brightly colored flowers blooming in all directions, and perfectly trimmed bushes. Suzanne particularly focuses on the unusual-looking birds. Their colors are spectacular. However, that's not what she notices most about them. They look as though they are talking to one another. Moreover, they look as if they are talking about her as if she is the talk of the town. She quickly shakes it off to her imagination.

'Surely birds are not talking about me,' she thought. 'It must be this head injury that is playing tricks on my mind. I am not right.' She feels strange. She chalks it up to her injuries and trauma. Still, she is in survival mode. Sightseeing mostly evades her consciousness. Reality keeps interrupting any moments of stasis she may have been experiencing. An acute stress response constantly reminds her that she is not where she needs to be. This distracts her from the moment and from really taking in her surroundings. For instance, it takes her some time to turn around and see a view of the plane she had just crash-landed in. When she does, the reality of the situation hits her like a ton of bricks.

She realizes she is most likely the only survivor of this horrific accident. However, she has no time to dwell on that. She needs to figure out where she is, and fast. She fails to notice the tiny, miniature houses behind her and to her left that have dome-shaped roofs. She also overlooks the myriad of little people hiding and peeking out from behind several structures, afraid and trying to remain unseen.

Suddenly, the wind begins stirring. Slowly at first, but steadily increasing in intensity. Leaves begin moving faster and faster from left to right, then in a circular motion. Within seconds, the wind is swirling so fast it is hard to see. Suzanne puts her right hand up, palm facing outward to cover her eyes. Loud crackling and fizzing sounds fill the air. Suzanne begins breathing tremulously. She opens one eye and looks out between her fingers. She sees lightning and sparks concentrated in an area just ahead of her. Loud, intense, thunderous crackling sounds continue, accompanied by an awe-inspiring light display and a rumbling of the ground. After reaching a crescendo, wind and electricity quickly decelerate.

Suzanne slowly removes her hand from her face and is astonished to see an older brunette woman standing just twenty feet in front of her.

The North Witch

The mysterious woman standing a few feet from Suzanne is dressed like an upscale gypsy in vintage boho-style clothing. She is an older, attractive woman sporting long brown hair (mixed with some greys) in a loop-waterfall-braid style.

"Hello, child," the woman says in a pleasant voice. "Are you ok?" Suzanne takes a second to assess herself. She stands up and gives herself a once-over.

"I-I think so," she responds. "Where am I? And who are you?"

"You are in *the land of Oz*, and I am

Zuri, the *North Witch;* ruler of the north."

"What the hell is Oz?" Suzanne asks in confusion. A chorus of snickers can be heard from all around. "What was that?" Suzanne asks nervously. The North Witch chuckles softly.

"Those are the residents of the area laughing at your humorous comment," she states.

"I don't see anyone," Suzanne replies. "And what's so funny? I truly have no idea where I am! I need help. I need to get home. I was in a plane crash, and I am the only survivor."

"I know, I see, dear," the woman responds while looking at the plane. "And you are very fortunate to be alive. Lucky indeed. Where have you come from?"

"I'm from *New Jersey.*"

"Well, that must be very, very far away as I've never heard such a phrase uttered before."

"Did you say you are a witch?" Suzanne asks.

"Yes, from the north," Zuri responds.

"Are there other witches around here as well?" Suzanne asks.

"Oh yes," Zuri responds. "A witch rules each of the four areas. I am the ruler of the north, and my sister, *Gwendolyn*, is the ruler of the south. The evilest of the witches rules the west. Her name is *Maura*. And her sister, who was a nasty old witch, *Jezebeth*, ruled the east where we currently are."

"Oh my God!" Suzanne mutters. "Is she gonna be mad that I am here?"

"Well, she would be," Zuri explains, "but you killed her."

"I what?" Suzanne shouts in confusion.

"You killed her," Zuri repeats. "Look, over there." She points to the plane. Underneath it is a left-arm sticking out almost to the shoulder and a bare left leg just under the knee. The left-hand ring finger bares a beautiful, thick ring that stands out because of its size. The rest of the body was crushed underneath the plane.

"Oh, my God!" Suzanne exclaims. "I am so sorry! I didn't mean to do that! I mean, I wasn't even flying the plane, so technically, I didn't do anything, but I swear, we didn't intend to kill anyone!" Zuri giggles again. She looks around briefly.

"You can come out now. It's safe." Slowly and reluctantly, little people, standing no more than three feet tall, reveal themselves in drones from every direction.

"Oh, my," Suzanne blurts out in shock. "I'm definitely not in Jersey anymore." Several titters from many of the little people are heard once more. Numerous little people cautiously approach the East Witch's body to confirm her death. One turns and shakes his head, confirming it to others. One of the little people creeps right up to her, yanks her bracelet off her wrist, and runs back into the crowd with it. People nearby cheer loudly.

"You have nothing to be sorry for," Zuri mentions. "In fact, we should be thanking you. You see, *Jezebeth*, there was a very evil witch. She practiced the dark arts. Together with her sister Maura, they terrorized this land for many years. Now, you have rid us of one of them and have tipped the balance of power into our favor." The tiny people start cheering!

"Well, you're welcome," Suzanne says reluctantly and humbly. "I'm happy I could help."

"You see, Jezebeth ruled this area by fear and intimidation. She held *Tiny Town* captive and treated the tiny people like slaves. She even rounded some of them up each month and shipped them off to the west, and they were never seen again."

"Why did she do that?" Suzanne asks.

"Because her sister commands a fearsome flying lion named *Gedeon*, and his favorite delicacy is tiny people."

"Oh, my Lord!" Suzanne cringes. "Wait, did you say a *flying lion*, like with wings?"

"Oh, yes," Zuri says matter-of-factly. "Why, you don't have flying lions in New Jersey?"

"Ahhh, no, we don't," Suzanne responds.

"Oh, it must be because it's new," Zuri replies. Suzanne shakes her head quickly, and her eyelids flutter at triple speed.

"Anyway," Suzanne says, "I really need to get back to school in California. No offense, but how the hell do I get out of here?"

"Well, your best bet is to go to *Emerald City* to see the *Wizard of Oz*," Zuri recommends. He is great and very powerful, and he too is a *Sky Person*."

"A Sky Person?" Suzanne asks.

"Yes, he fell from the sky as you did. But he is a powerful Wizard from your land, and he should be able to help you."

"Umm, we don't have any wizards, but ok, great! How do I get there?" Suzanne asks, relieved.

"Oh," Zuri chuckles again, as do the tiny people. "It will be dark out soon. You do not want to travel through these woods in the dark, I tell you." Suddenly, a little person dressed in a three-piece suit approaches Suzanne.

"Hello, madame," the man says. "I am *Chester*, the mayor of *Tiny Town*. I would like to sincerely thank you for freeing our people! We would like to invite you to a feast tonight in your honor!" Everyone starts cheering.

"Oh, no, no, I can't," Suzanne responds. "I must get home."

"You are welcome to stay the night with us, and we will show you the way to the *Emerald City* in the morning," Chester explains.

"How far is the Emerald City from here?" Suzanne asks.

"It's a few days' walk from here," Zuri replies.

"Oh, shit!" Suzanne cries. "Ok, I'm pretty hungry. I could use some good food and water." More cheers ring out as they lead Suzanne to her sleeping quarters to freshen up before the feast. The ceilings in the homes in Tiny Town are six-feet high. Thankfully, Suzanne is only five-feet-five inches tall, so she is able to navigate comfortably within these confines. Although, she does need to duck down to avoid hitting her head on the doorway arches.

The Tiny Town Feast

The feast was prepared on short notice. All the cooks, maids, waiters, and waitresses—and anyone else involved in organizing this gala event—were scrambling to prepare things. They would use the large auditorium for the event. Every cook in the town raced to prepare the food. Tables had to be set up; signs had to be made. All hands were on deck. All of the distinguished members of Tiny Town would be in attendance. But most importantly, Zury and Gwendolyn would be there as well.

There weren't any clothes readily available that would fit Suzanne, so Zuri cooked up a spell and provided her with the most beautiful dress for the occasion. Zuri even provided her with a deep wardrobe, aside from what was in Suzanne's carry-on duffle bag. For the event, Suzanne wore a silver cape dress with an open back and hood that fanned out wide at the bottom, just touching the floor as she walked. Everyone "oohed and aahed" as Suzanne entered the auditorium. She was treated like a queen right from the start. The maître d' escorted Suzanne to her table, which was upfront at the guest of honor table. She would sit with all of the important people of Tiny Town, including Chester (the Mayor), Gwendolyn, and Zuri.

Gwendolyn was the first to approach her.

"I've heard so many good things about you in the short time you have been here," she says. "I am *Gwendolyn*, the ruler of the south."

"It is a pleasure to make your acquaintance, your highness," Suzanne replies with a curtsy. Gwendolyn giggles fondly at the gesture.

"You do not need to greet me in such a formal way," she says. "We are on equal ground here. You have done us all a great service, and we are here tonight to honor you."

"I am more than grateful for such an honor," Suzanne replies. "What should I call you?"

"You can call me Gwendolyn."

"I feel a little funny doing so since

you are such a highly exalted ruler here, and I am a newcomer, but if you insist."

"I do," Gwendolyn mentions.

"Everyone take your seats, please," someone says on the microphone on stage, which is about a foot off the ground. Suzanne takes her seat next to *Cricket*, the head banker of the town. "We would like to start the festivities. And to do so, I would like to introduce the mayor of Tiny Town, *Chester Vestor*. The crowd applauds fervently for their very popular and well-liked mayor. Chester shakes hands with his announcer and grabs the microphone.

"Ladies and gentlemen, this is a special event today. In fact, it is the most special event that this town has ever witnessed!" The crowd applauds. It is an emotional, electric atmosphere. "For decades, we have endured the oppression, abuse, and down-right slaughter of our people at the hands of the East Witch and her family. For many years, we have heard of the prophecy from the Wizard that a Sky Person would come and defeat the East Witch. We grew sour on him after a while because we started to doubt that he was a true prophet. But tonight, I can finally stand here and say, with complete confidence, that the Wizard is indeed whom he says he is, all-powerful; all-knowing!" More cheers fill the room.

"But as much as we owe the Wizard for doubting him and helping us keep the faith for so long in the face of tyranny, we owe even more to the person who has ended our suffering!" The crowd cheers the loudest thus far. The crowd starts chanting low at first, "*Suzanne, Suzanne, Suzanne,*" then gradually gets louder and louder until it reaches a climax. The mayor halts the chanting once it has peaked with a hand gesture. "And so right now, I want to call someone to the stage that has unfettered Tiny Town from the clutches of despotism! Future generations will speak of this moment as the turning point in our history. And our children and their children will never have to go through the atrocities that we had to in order to survive!"

Everyone stands up and applauds ardently. Several members of the audience have tears in their eyes. Suzanne looks around, not sure what to do. She stands but is overwhelmed by the moment. It is so surreal that she forgot that the speech was even about her. Cricket nudges her and gives her a head nod to go onstage. Suzanne stops clapping, points to herself, and mouths the word, "Me?" Cricket shakes his head up and down and nudges her gently. Suzanne halfheartedly walks onstage. A few hours ago, she was on a plane headed back to college that crashed and killed everyone onboard except her, and now she is a hero because the plane she was a passenger on crashed and killed the evil ruler of this mysterious village and freed the people, to which she is getting credit for orchestrating. To say the moment is surreal would be an understatement.

When she arrives onstage, the mayor turns to her. The applause stop and people again take their seats.

"Suzanne, in honor of what you did for our precious people and land, we give you this as a token of our appreciation!" the crowd again provides a standing ovation. The mayor holds out a ring, offering it to Suzanne.

"I can't accept this, mister mayor,"

she says. "I did not do anything extraordinary to deserve this."

"Oh no, no, no, you don't understand," the mayor says. "You must take this ring?"

"Why do you say it like that?" she asks.

"It will protect you from the *West Witch*. Because when she finds out that you killed her sister, she will come for you and kill you in the worst way you could ever imagine." The mayor grabs her hand and slides the ring on her finger. Suzanne has a blank stare on her face. She is confused and scared by the mayor's unexpected directness, but she remains calm on the outside and goes with the moment. She returns to her seat to another standing ovation. Music starts to play, and drinks are soon served.

Gwendolyn is seated at the head of the long table. Zuri sits at the head on the other end. Suzanne sits in the middle of the table with Cricket to her right. The food is served in courses. The plating of the food is impeccably arranged.

"Thank you for helping me before,"

Suzanne says to *Cricket*.

"The thanks should be from us," he replies. "This must be a bit of culture shock for you?"

"Ya think?" Suzanne responds.

"I do," he replies.

"No, I meant that sarcastically, like yeah, very much," she explains.

"Ah, yes, sarcasm," he says. "I am quite sarcastic myself. I am just not used to people understanding or responding to mine. People in this town are so by-the-book. From the way they speak to the way they act. Hopefully, people will loosen up a bit now that you have killed the Witch!"

"Tell me about this place?" Suzanne asks.

"What do you mean?" Cricket responds.

"What's the deal with the witches? I assume Gwendolyn and Zuri are good, and the others are bad. How did this all come to be?"

"This struggle has been going on for many years," Cricket explains. "Zuri and Gwendolyn are sisters from a family that has ruled the north and south for centuries.

Similarly, the east and west witches come from a competing royal family. There was once peace in the land between all factions. This place was paradise. But somewhere along the line, the east-west family stopped practicing *White Magic* and started dabbling in *Dark Sorcery*. It didn't take long for the darkness to seduce them. After that, they became monsters consumed with power and control. Over the years, all the good has been bread out of them. All they know is evil. I don't envy you."

"What do you mean?" Suzanne asks.

"That ring will certainly help you, but when the *West Witch* finds out about what you did to her sister, she will stop at nothing to possess and torture you. And that dark magic is very tricky. Moreover, Maura is the most powerful of all the witches, even more powerful than Gwendolyn. You best not trust anyone once you leave this place."

"Oh, great!" Suzanne utters. "Just my luck to have an evil witch trying to kill me for something I didn't do. I'm so over this place already. I need another drink. Wanna do a shot with me?"

"A shot?" Cricket asks.

"Yeah, like, you pour a small drink and then drink it really fast."

"Isn't that bad for the digestive system?" Cricket asks.

"Live a little, Cricket! Your people are free for the first time in however long. Plus, I'm the guest of honor, and I command you to do a shot with me! Shit, if I'm gonna die anyway, I might as well live it up tonight." Cricket shrugs his shoulders and goes along with Suzanne's command.

The mayor's wife walks over just after Suzanne and Cricket kick back the shots.

"Have any of you seen *Shorty*?" she asks. Everyone says no. "If any of you see him, please tell him to come see me immediately." She walks off and finds the mayor. "I can't find *Shorty*," she says, sounding a bit unnerved.

"He is probably at a brothel drinking and fornicating," his father responds. "I swear, that boy will be the death of me!"

"You need to put your personal feelings aside right now," she says.

"Don't worry," he replies. "He will turn up tomorrow hung over and asking for money," Chester says with contempt.

"I've been meaning to ask, why do they call you Cricket?" Suzanne asks.

"Funny story," he replies, looking slightly embarrassed. "I have a bearded dragon as a pet. They like to eat crickets. One day I decided to order a bunch of crickets to be sent by mail. I received a big box. There must have been more than three hundred crickets inside. I didn't want to open it right away, but I didn't want them to suffocate. Plus, I have two cats, and I didn't want them feasting on them. So, I put the box in the upstairs bathroom and cut a small hole in it for ventilation. I thought a few would get out, but no big deal. I go into the kitchen like twenty minutes later and find a bunch of crickets jumping around. I decided to go check the upstairs bathroom. As I got to the stairs, I noticed it was filled with crickets. When I got upstairs and opened the bathroom door, there were crickets everywhere. It took me all night to gather them all. And so, the name stuck after people heard about it." Suzanne starts laughing. "I'm just lucky my wife is still with me after all of that."

They have several more drinks as the night goes on. Suzanne gets up and gets on the dance floor. "Come dance with me!" she commands of Cricket. There are no percussion instruments in the music. Suzanne runs on stage and quickly teaches one of the musicians how to hold a beat by stomping his feet in rhythm. Many in the crowd follow along. Once the beat is established, she shows them how she dances in the clubs in Jersey. At first, her dancing seems strange. Suzanne danced like she was listening to a *Little John* song. However, many of the little people started mimicking her moves. Suzanne announced several toasts throughout the night as well. Many of the town's residents got drunker than they had ever been, but everyone had a blast, including Suzanne, who was quite drunk, herself.

Chapter 3 – The Tin Soldier

The Tin Soldier & The Campers

That night, as Suzanne and the rest of *Tiny Town* went to bed, several miles away in the southwest section of Oz, three *Sky People* dressed in *US Military* uniforms and one tiny person were sitting at a campfire eating some strange type of bird they had just cooked. They were having an informative discussion about recent events. They are in full camouflage, carrying modern military weapons and supplies witnessed in the US.

"You are telling me the *East Witch* was killed today after getting hit by a plane, *Shorty*?" *Mariette* asks.

"Yes, she called it a plane," Shorty replies. "It was a long tubular object with what she called wings. She said she was from the *New Jersey*."

"That's where *Rodriguez* is from, New Jersey!" *Gonzales* interjects.

"And you are sure that witch, or

43

whoever, said the Wizard guy in Emerald City can help her get home?" *Mariette* asks.

"That's what the North Witch suggested," Shorty responds.

"Can you take us to this Wizard guy?" *Murphy* asks.

"For a fee, sure," Shorty replies.

"Whatever you want, Shorty, no problem," Mariette responds.

"I can't fucking believe this," Gonzales says. "We have been here for almost two months, and we finally stumble upon this little guy."

"I told you fucking guys that I heard about those wormholes," Mariette asserts. "Now we know for sure that a fucking plane from our world, New Jersey, to be exact, landed in this fucked up nightmare!"

"I still think it's some type of time machine," Gonzalez says.

"Or maybe a fucking top-secret portal of some kind," Murphy asserts. "Whatever it is, I say we get some rest tonight and head out first thing in the morning to see this Wizard guy," Murphy suggests.

"Sounds like a plan," Mariette replies.

"Yes, we are finally getting out of this

place! *F-Troop!*" Gonzalez shouts.

"*F-Troop!*" they all shout in unison.

Just then, several hard, metallic thumping sounds can be heard in the distance that are repeating rhythmically.

Clang, clang...

"What the fuck is that?" Mariette asks the group.

"Sounds like a fucking jackhammer in slow motion," Murphy responds.

"Shorty, do you know what that is?" Mariette asks in a slight panic as the sound grows louder.

"I don't know," Shorty responds. "This is the first time I have been out of Tiny Town. But it can't be good. I have heard stories of a *Tin Soldier* who is the enforcer for the West Witch. Like, her right-hand hitman. I'm just hoping it's not him!"

"Ok, let's spread out and take cover," Mariette orders. "Keep your radios on channel eleven and report anything you see. Shorty, you're with me." Gonzales runs off to the right and lies down on a small hill about twenty-yards east of the campsite. Murphy heads to the left and kneels behind a thick tree about 15 yards west of the camping grounds. Mariette and Shorty hide in the bushes just behind the campsite. "Confirm your positions?" Mariette commands. They all relay their locations via the radio a few seconds later. Mariette then orders radio silence until the object causing the disturbance is located. Suddenly, the sound stops.

Other than the sounds of a few howling wolves and insects chittering, there is silence. After about five minutes, the group gets restless. Gonzales is lying on his stomach, looking through his sniper scope, slowly surveying the area. They all have night-vision equipped. Gonzales sees movement as he scans the area. He is unable to determine the source of the movement. It was a blur, but his instinct tells him it was some sort of stealthy move from someone who knows he is being tracked. He grabs his radio. "*Ghost Team*, this is *Bronx*. Movement of unconfirmed object twenty-yards north-east of zero [campsite]."

"Bronx, this is *Austin* [Mariette]. Hold your position and report further when the target is located."

"Roger that," Gonzales responds. Gonzales resumes perusing the area through his scope. He is on high alert and scanning the area with his scope much faster than before. A few more minutes go by with nothing noteworthy to report. Then, Gonzales hears the *'clanging'* sound briefly behind him. Caught off guard, he turns quickly. His mouth and eyes open wide. His heart races. He puts both hands over his face with increased muscle tension. The *Tin Soldier*, standing six feet, six inches tall, has his ax raised high above his head, holding it with both hands. His mechanical eyes are red, his face is expressionless, his tin-body looks like a chiseled body-builder, and his head is bald, round, and tin as well. He is truly a menacing presence. He brings the ax down with extreme force. Gonzales screams in terror, "No!!!" The ax rips through Gonzales's head, splitting it in two. Blood spatters all about. The ax is stuck in the dirt. The *Tin Soldier* puts his right foot on Gonzales's chest and pulls the ax from the ground. Gonzales is barely recognizable after the fierce blow.

"What the fuck was that?" Mariette

utters. Shorty is shaking with hunched shoulders, looking around fearfully. "Bronx, this is Austin, report!" He waits a few seconds but gets no response. "Bronx, this is Austin; report now!" A few more seconds go by, but no response. Mariette is having trouble swallowing. His mouth goes dry. "*Memphis* (Murphy), this is Austin. Did you hear a noise?"

"Austin, this is Memphis, sounded like Gonzales screaming. It didn't sound good. Want me to check on him?"

"No, I'm closer. I will go check. Stay sharp! Shorty, stay close. If anything happens, run and don't look back." Shorty begins trembling as he shakes his head up and down in compliance. Mariette moves cautiously toward Gonzales's last known location. His rifle is drawn and ready to engage.

Murphy is holding his position when he hears a loud 'clank' behind him from the south side. He looks into the vast array of trees and bushes but cannot see very far.

"Who's there?" he shouts. After a few seconds, he turns back to facing north.

Thump!

Murphy's back is struck by an acorn. He turns back quickly, ready to fire. He looks to the ground and sees the acorn that hit him. He looks up and sees a tree full of acorns above. He smirks and turns back around.

Bam!

This time, an acorn hits him in the back of the head at high velocity. He turns again. "What the fuck!?" he shouts in frustration. He sees no one. However, he realizes that no acorn falling from above could have hit him in the back of the head with such force. "Yo, whoever is out there better come out right now!" he yells as he slowly walks south. "I got an *M4 Carbine* in hand right now. I know you backward asses don't know what that is, but I assure you, it will shred twenty-men in seconds!" He fires a few shots in the air for effect. A call comes in on his radio a few seconds later.

"Memphis, this is Austin. I heard shots fired, report!" Murphy turns the volume off on his radio and proceeds forward.

"It's just you and me, Fella!" Murphy proclaims. He walks forward. Murphy's feet crackle tree branches and crunch dry leaves. As he walks past a tree, he ducks quickly. A whooshing sound is heard as an ax barely misses the top of his head. Murphy raises back up and begins firing.

Bang, bang, bang!

He shoots three holes through the chest of the Tin Soldier, who doesn't flinch. Instead, it grabs the barrel of the gun and raises it up. Another shot fires into the air. The Tin Soldier pulls on the barrel and dislodges the gun from Murphy's hands. It tosses Murphy's gun over its right shoulder. Murphy is beyond perplexed when he sees three bullet holes through the chest of this machine, and yet, it is not only still standing, it is moving toward him, unphased and in an aggressive fashion. Murphy has been in numerous combat situations and has never been rattled until now.

The Tin Soldier grabs Murphy by the neck, raises him off his feet, and tightens his grip. Murphy tries desperately to loosen its grip. He swings his right and left arms desperately at the right arm of his assailant to no avail. Murphy struggles to take a breath. The veins in his neck are popping out. Murphy gasps for air. His eyelids start slowly closing as he loses consciousness. The Tin Soldier tosses Murphy backward about five yards like a rag doll. Murphy lands on his back, momentarily unconscious. He quickly awakens and puts his hands on his neck while clenching his face and retching. There is no quit in Murphy. He knows he must get to his feet and find a way to combat this unknown attacker.

Not seeing Murphy as a threat whatsoever, the Tin Soldier slowly walks away from him to retrieve his ax. Murphy takes this time to grab a grenade off his belt. He pulls the pin and throws it at the tin monster.

Boom!

Smoke, dirt, and other debris fill the air. Murphy looks desperately for any sign that he has finished off the alien enemy. As the smoke begins to subside, the Tin Soldier comes into view. He is standing there with his ax in hand, unphased. The brief offensive only seems to anger it. The tin creature walks aggressively toward Murphy, who is still lying on his back. It raises the ax and strikes him on the leg, severing his leg from the rest of his body. Murphy screams in agony and begins tearing up as he looks at his detached leg. Murphy groans and pants while holding the remains of his leg with both hands. The Tin Soldier grabs his severed leg by the ankle. He swings it at Murphy's face several times, essentially beating him to death with his own leg.

****

A few minutes earlier, Mariette and Shorty approach the last known location of Gonzales.

"Gonzales!" Mariette shouts. "Where are you?" Not long into their search, they see a body dressed in US Army fatigues in the distance. "Gonzales, are you ok?" Mariette shouts, sounding somewhat relieved. However, as he gets closer, he sees a gruesome sight. At first, he thinks his eyes are playing tricks on him. However, it is soon apparent that Gonzales had been butchered. "Oh, fuck!" Mariette shouts. "Who the fuck did this?!"

"It had to be the West Witches' people," Shorty replies. "We are as good as dead right now. You don't know what we are dealing with!" Shorty starts panicking. "I should have never left Tiny Town! This is going to kill my parents!"

"Hold on, hold on," Mariette says. "We are not dying today!"

"You don't understand," Shorty replies, tears falling from his eyes.

"Just stay close, Shorty," Mariette warns. "We are gonna make it out of this!" Just then, they hear a shot fired.

Bang!

"What the fuck was that?!" Mariette yells. He grabs his radio. "Memphis, this is Austin. I heard shots fired, report!" He gets no answer. He tries again, "Memphis, this is Austin. I heard shots fired, report!" He still receives no response.

"We need to go check on Murphy!" Mariette says.

"No, no, we need to run!" Shorty shouts.

"I cannot abandon anyone in my squad," Mariette explains.

"I'm out of here!" Shorty affirms. He

turns and runs in the opposite direction. Mariette heads toward the last known location of Murphy.

Bang, bang, bang!

He hears three more shots coming from the area where Murphy was positioned. Mariette starts running furiously in that direction. Seconds later, he hears another shot!

"Murph!" he screams but gets no reply. He decides to remain quiet from that point on in case the enemy has overwhelmed Murphy. He did not want to give them easy access to his location. He walks forward cautiously. He looks to his right and sees a good amount of blood on some bushes. He is an expert tracker. He follows the blood trail. He doesn't have to go far before he comes upon Murphy's body hanging from a tree branch by the strap of his own gun with his leg missing. Mariette is horrified! He has no idea who or how many enemies are out there.

Furthermore, he was the leader of this special ops team. They were the best of the best. They had been through many dangerous operations together, some with impossible odds, yet, they had always managed to get the job done. Moreover, even in the face of the most extreme circumstances, outnumbered and all, they knew they were so good that they never feared mission failure. For Mariette to see his top soldiers taken down in such a humiliating way made him question what were they up against.

Mariette wouldn't have to wait long to find out. As he was looking at Murphy's body in a state of confusion, the Tin Soldier walked up behind him.

Clang, clang!

Mariette hears the sounds and knows the enemy is behind him. The Tin Soldier charges. Mariette turns quickly and fires simultaneously.

Bang!

The Tin Soldier pushed the barrel of the gun to its left. The bullet narrowly misses the monster. It elbows Mariette in his face causing him to inadvertently drops his weapon and stumble backward. The Tin Soldier takes a few steps forward. Mariette's gun is now behind his enemy, so he pulls out two large serrated knives from his belt area.

"Ok, you shit-can' you're expired, bitch! Let's do this!" The Tin Soldier charges again. The Tin Soldier swings its ax with fury. Mariette uses his speed to side-step the blow while simultaneously sliding both blades across the machine's *left knee*. The strike dislodged the knee a bit, causing a slight limp. However, this only seems to further anger the Tin Soldier. It again rushes in for the attack, swinging the ax from left to right. Mariette ducks. The Tin Soldier quickly grabs the ax with both hands and raises it over its head. It brings it down with great force. Mariette rolls forward between its legs and pops up behind the monster as it brings the ax down. Mariette plunges his knife into its neck with his right hand and then yanks it out. He then stabs it in the left side of its head with his left hand then pulls out the knife. Sparks fly. The Tin Soldier spins quickly, swinging its right arm backward, striking Mariette in his jaw. The blow sends him flying onto his back, rendering him unconscious for a few seconds.

When Mariette opens his eyes, he

notices that he is tied to a tree by a sturdy rope. He struggles to get loose to no avail. He looks up and sees *Shorty* tied to a tree across from him. Shorty looks bad. His face is heavily bruised, and he is barely conscious.

"Shorty?" Mariette whispers. "Are you ok?" Shorty doesn't respond. The Tin Soldier walks over seconds later and grabs Shorty by his chin, waking him up momentarily. It points its ax at Mariette and then walks over to him. The Tin Soldier looks back at Shorty, then swings the ax with fury. The ax strikes Mariette in his neck. The force is so strong that it goes through Mariette's neck and sticks firmly into the tree. Mariette's head bounces off the tree and rolls to the feet of Shorty. As Shorty looks down, he sees Mariette's eyes staring back at him with his mouth open and a frightened look frozen on his face.

Chapter 4 – The West Witch Strikes Back

No "Maura" Nonsense

At dawn, the birds are happily chirping, and roosters are crowing contently. It appears to be a very peaceful morning. However, the irony of the situation is that the peaceful appearance is only an illusion. The fresh stench of death is in the air as the Tin Soldier methodically drags two large heavy-duty black plastic bags along the ground, one in each hand. Something inside the left bag appears to be moving or squirming around periodically. It drags the bags all the way up the steep mountainside until it comes upon an entrance near the top of the mountain. It is, indeed, the *West Witch's Lair*. The Tin Soldier drags the bodies through several corridors until it reaches a room with a sizeable *white pentagram* on the ground, and the West Witch standing in the middle of it. She is involved in some sort of ritual, her eyes closed in deep meditation. However, a *tall hooded figure* stands to her left who appears to be whispering in her ear, almost as if he is in charge. The hood covers his face. When he feels the presence of the Tin Soldier approaching, he quickly scurries out of the room unseen.

The West Witch, *Maura*, not only has a terrifying personality but also looks frightening as well. She has straight jet-black hair with a ghostly white complexion. Her pupils are black, her scleras are white, and her irises are off-white. Maura's face appears decayed, much like that of a zombie. There are cracks on her face from dryness, and her lips are dry and chapped. She has black hyperpigmentation under both eyes (the eye orbits). It almost looks like she is wearing black makeup under her eyes. Maura is long and lean, standing nearly six feet tall. She is wearing a black crushed velvet dress, fitted over the bust and waist, with an off-shoulder neckline. The skirt flares from the waist into a long, flowing, bias-cut skirt.

The Tin Soldier drops the bags on the rocky mountain floor. This breaks the witch out of her comatose state.

"And what do we have here?" she asks delightfully as she steps outside the pentagram. Her voice is deep, dark, and raspy. The Tin Soldier reaches in one of the bags and pulls Shorty out by his collar. Shorty shakes in terror when he sees the West Witch. *The lion*, restrained by a chain around his neck attached to the cave wall, roars with fury once he sees and smells Shorty. The lion briskly charges Shorty, only to be sharply halted as the chain has reached its limit. He can hardly contain himself as little people are his favorite delicacy. Tiny bones are scattered all around him. He raises his head and begins sniffing for Shorty's scent.

The lion is an intimidating creature. He has large wings attached to what appears to be two thin, long arms protruding out of his back. At the end of each arm is a single black hooked claw. He also has a stinger at the end of his tail, identical to a scorpion that can inject its prey with highly venomous poison, similar in potency to cyanide. He is three times larger than a normal-sized male lion, and his bite is twice as strong. He has long hair covering his head and neck and a beard and mustache. His face looks eerily similar to a human face.

"Well, well," the witch gushes. "I didn't expect such a treat." Shorty is breathing shakily and sweating. "Why have you wandered so far home, little one?"

"There-there is a celebration going on in Tiny Town, and I was able to slip away unseen," Shorty blurts out.

"A celebration?" the witch says in confusion. "I have not heard of any celebration planned. Surely, I would have heard of such a thing. My sister would never allow such a thing!"

"With all due respect, Miss Witch, that celebration is because of your sister," Shorty explains.

"Because of her?" the witch asks.

"Yes," Shorty relays. "She was killed by a metal bird in the sky that crashed into Tiny Town." The witch's eyes open wide, and her demeanor changes quickly into an agitated state.

"She what?!" the witch shouts. "The East Witch is dead, you say?"

"Yes, and the celebration was for the woman who killed her, a sky person named Suzanne," Shorty elucidates. The witch pauses for a moment.

"Are you sure?" the witch says as she walks closer to Shorty, leans over, and stares into his eyes. "You wouldn't be trying to trick me, now would ya?"

"Oh no, no, ma'am. I swear! She is dead. I saw her body under the object. It must have weighed tons." Maura turns away from Shorty, grief-stricken.

"Oh," the witch cries. "Oh, oh, my poor sister! Poor Jezebeth!" Maura turns back and faces Shorty. "Tell me more, and I will let you live. Where is this woman who killed my sister?"

"Zuri told her to walk the Yellow Brick Road to see the Wizard. She said he will help her get home."

"Home, eh?!" the witch jeers. She raises her right hand. Even though she is not touching Shorty, he raises off of the ground in unison with her hand. She quickly moves her hand to her right, and Shorty flies in the air in the direction her hand had moved.

"Woh!" Shorty screams. The lion jumps in the air and flaps his wings slightly, leaving him suspended in air for a few moments. The lion catches Shorty with his teeth while in midair. Shorty screams as the first two bites from the lion sink deep into his flesh. The third bite to his neck silences him for good. The witch paces back and forth, oblivious to the grunts and growls of the lion as the sound of him tearing through flesh and crushing bones is almost deafening.

"I must confirm that what he said is true," the witch states. "She grabs a few body parts from the other bag: a leg, an arm, and a head. She dumps them into the large boiling cauldron with only God knows what else. Two of the witch's soldiers take the remaining body parts out of the bag and hang them in the back with meat hooks. She stirs and mixes the concoction with a large four-foot wooden spoon. "Rotting meat, rotting meat, show me my sister's defeat. Bethy rewop othef ecrous. Tangr em scesac!" Suddenly, she sees her sister's dead body, Suzanne being handed her sister's ring by the mayor of Tiny Town, and all the happy people in Tiny Town drinking and dancing. The images only manage to infuriate her further.

"I will avenge your death, sister!" the witch promises. "They have no idea the wrath I will bring upon them for this! And this Suzanne girl; I want her brought to me alive! I will rip her limb from limb, turn her into a frog, and have her live out eternity being eaten and hunter. She will not have one full day of rest for the remainder of eternity!" She turns to the Tin Soldier. "Continue to kill every sky person you see and capture any little person alive. Get as much information out of them as you can before you kill them!"

The Yellow Brick Road

Suzanne is sound asleep on her back. Her legs, from the middle of her caves to her feet, hang off the end of the tiny bed. The morning light shines through the unusually small window. She twitches once, then turns on her left side. Moments later, she turns to her right side before turning onto her back. Then, her eyes open.

"Damn, what a crazy dream," she says aloud. She is a bit hung over from the previous night's festivities. She lies there for a few moments, rehashing some of the events of her strange dream. Then, she feels a pain in her caves. She sits up and rests her feet on the floor on the side of the bed. She is dizzy at first. "I wonder what mother cooked for breakfast?" she says. The room suddenly comes into focus. She lets out a loud scream! She sees a tiny room, with a tiny dresser, and a tiny mirror on top. She jumps out of bed and looks out of the unusually small window. She sees scores of little people gathered around a trail of yellow-covered bricks coiled around a similar trail of red bricks. "It was real?" she asks herself in confusion.

Suzanne looks at her clothing. She is wearing pajamas, a matching shirt, and elastic waistband pants, white with a blue flower theme. She sees a set of clothes folded on top of the tiny dresser. She grabs them and looks them over. She picks up a white short-shirt off the neck. Next, she finds a pair of jeans ripped over both thighs and on one knee, folded up at the bottom with a thick belt for the waist. She looks on the floor and sees a pair of white tennis sneakers.

She gets dressed and hurries outside. Gwendolyn and Zuri are among the many that are there to greet her. They cheer as she comes into view.

"What's going on?" Suzanne asks.

"We are here to see you off," Zuri replies.

"You need to go see the Wizard to get home," Gwendolyn explains, "and to do so, you must follow the *Yellow Brick Road*." She points down.

"How long is the trip?" Suzanne asks.

"It should take you a day or two," Zuri explains.

"Is it safe?" Suzanne asks.

"Not if the West Witch finds out you killed her sister, it won't be," Gwendolyn responds.

"Oh, great!" Suzanne says in frustration. "Well, I don't have much of a choice, I guess."

"Just remember to never remove the

East Witch's ring," Gwendolyn warns. "It will protect you from the West Witch. And always follow this road!"

"Ok, well, here goes nothing," Suzanne says. She begins following the trail. After a few steps, she turns and looks back. Gwendolyn gestures for her to continue forward. Suzanne turns reluctantly and continues on. The town waves her off and cheers as she slowly moves out of sight.

You've Got a Friend

Suzanne walked the road alone for hours. She was excited at first as she saw so many beautiful sights she had never seen before. She witnessed succulent fruits hanging neatly from the trees lining the road. She sees a horde of tiny flying lights, no bigger than gnats but just balls of light flying in circles near the road. As she approaches them, they scatter about quickly and out of sight. She is also perplexed by a frog-like creature that she sees walking upright on its two hind legs. She stops and stares in awe. As soon as the creature notices her, it scurries off into the woods.

However, after a few hours, her attention shifts abruptly from the aesthetic beauty of the area to the long journey she has ahead. Her legs and calves start to tighten. A desire for food and drink creep into her mind. How would she eat? Where would she find water? These things she had not thought of before leaving *Tiny Town*. She only thought of returning home. Now, she is faced with the reality of the moment. Moreover, she would need to endure this road alone for at least another day or two. That would mean she would need to stop focusing on the future and start thinking about how she would find her next meal or next drink of water.

It all hit her at once, the gravity and reality of the situation. She stopped and began to cry. For the first time, thoughts that she may never see home again crept into her mind. That's when she heard a short whistling sound. She stopped and looked around. Trees and bushes lined the road of the dense forest. It was hard to see twenty feet off the road. She continued on. However, the brief whistling sounded again after she took a few more steps. It was definitely not a bird, she thought. It was a familiar type of whistle. One she had heard before. She looked to her right and saw something move quickly behind some bushes. It looked like someone's head.

"Who is there?" she shouts. She receives no response. She waits in silence for a few moments, staring at the location she believes she saw the movement. The whistle sounds again. She is sure this time that it came from the same area where her eyes are focusing. "I hear you," she shouts. "Show yourself, you coward!" She walks into the brush and toward the area where she thought the sound was coming from. After a few steps in, she hears bushes rustling to her right. She runs toward the sound. "Come out now!" she commands. "I hear you!" She walks a few more steps forward and sees a pair of eyes staring at her nervously behind a nearby bush. "I see you," she says calmly. "I am not going to hurt you. Please show yourself. You are scaring me."

Seconds later, a *Black male* rises slowly from behind a thick bush. He stands nearly six feet six inches tall. He has a medium-sized afro and is lanky yet muscularly defined.

"Who are you?" he asks defensively.

"I am Suzanne Millington. Who are you?"

"I am *Henry Moore*."

"Where are you from, Henry?"

"I am not from here, that's for sure. What about you?"

"Me neither," Suzanne replies. "I am from *New Jersey*, a land far from here."

"I have a cousin there," Henry responds politely, "from Paterson."

"Really?" she replies excitedly. "I was on my way back to *UCLA,* where I go to school, and my plane crashed and somehow landed here."

"You gotta be kidding me?!" Henry exclaims.

"I'm not; why?"

"Because I am a freshman at UCLA!" Henry explains. "I was a *blue-chip* high school basketball player highly recruited by the Bruins from Florida. Go, *Bruins*! Ohhhh!" Henry extends the 'Oh,' and Suzanne joins in. They both clap quickly eight times while counting each clap out loud. After the eighth clap, they both shout "U." They immediately clap three more times rapidly, then shout "C." They repeat the three claps and shout, "LLLL (extending the 'L' sound)." Three more fast claps, and they yell, "A." Then finish by both yelling, "UCLA, FIGHT, FIGHT, FIGHT!" This clearly validates that they are both attendees of the school.

"No way!?" Suzanne says. "How the hell did you end up here?"

"I was on a private jet headed back to school. I'm not sure how we got here, but after we landed, we tried to figure out where we were. I was with three people. Then, while I was off taking a piss, some evil robot with an ax came out of nowhere and brutally murdered the three people I was with. I hid and have been hiding ever since. You should have seen this thing! It looked like a terminator or something."

"How long have you been here?" Suzanne asks.

"About a week," he replies. "Do you have any idea where we are or what's going on?"

"Not really," she says. "But I have become friendly with a few locals, and they told me that our way out is with the Wizard in Emerald City."

"The who?" he asks.

"I was given specific instructions to follow this *Yellow Brick Road* to the Emerald City to speak with the Wizard. They said he can help me get home. Would you like to join me?"

"I don't know," Henry says. "How do you know these people aren't leading you astray?"

"Well, they fed me, gave me shelter, and were very good to me," Suzanne expressed. "Do you have a better plan than hiding in the bushes for the rest of your life?"

"Ok, well, I guess we need to follow the Yellow Brick Road then," Henry pronounces.

"Are you with me?" Suzanne asks firmly. "I'm not looking to partner up with someone who is gonna run off at the first sign of trouble."

"I'm all in!" Henry states. "Let's do this!" They both walk the path together on their way to see the Wizard.

****

They both walked the Yellow Brick Road. At first, they just looked around, fearing what was out there. However, after about ten minutes, they settled in and took comfort in the fact that they were no longer alone.

"So, what year are you at UCLA?" Suzanne asks.

"I am a freshman," Henry says. I was a *blue-chip* athlete in high school and got a full scholarship to play basketball at UCLA."

"Oh, wow!" Suzanne says excitedly. "So, you must be a pretty good basketball player. You sure are tall enough!" Henry stands at six-feet-six-inches tall, towering over the five-foot-five Suzanne. "What does *blue-chip* mean?"

"Every year, they pick the best high school basketball players in the country to be recruited by the top colleges," Henry replies. "If you are deemed a 'blue-chip player,' you are one of the top high school prospects in the country."

"Wow, sounds like you have a bright future!" Suzanne mentions forgetting where they are.

"Maybe if I was back home," Henry says. "But here, it seems like we have no future at all!" Henry's statement brings Suzanne back to reality, temporarily putting her in a somber mental space. "Honestly, though, I have been feeling overwhelmed since I got to UCLA. I am not sure I am even gonna make it." His statement snaps Suzanne out of her funk.

"What do you mean?" she asks.

"I'm not really good at academics and tests and stuff," Henry announces.

"You just have to study and apply yourself, just like everyone else," Suzanne suggests.

"I think I might have a brain deficiency or something," Henry mentions. "At least that's what my father always tells me. I just can't seem to work out the problems in school put before me."

"Maybe you just need some guidance or a tooter?" Suzanne recommends. "Plus, school is not for everyone. A lot of people who struggled in school become very successful in life."

"Yeah, well, that sounds good, but maybe I'm lacking brains," Henry says. "I'm just not comfortable or secure making decisions in an academic setting."

"Well, academic settings don't always translate to real-life settings," Suzanne states. "Maybe you just need to find yourself outside of that area. Also, you might be putting undue emphasis on the academic aspect, like psyching yourself out."

"You might be right," Henry says. "Thank you for the vote of encouragement. Most people just say I'm not that bright."

"Yeah, well, I wouldn't put too much stock into what people think," Suzanne emphasizes. "Group mentality often basis decisions on societal biases or superficial presuppositions."

"I agree," Henry affirms. "I always say that people don't really understand me. They look at the color of my skin and my height and just assume I am a dumb jock. I guess after being perceived that way for so many years, I just accepted that as truth. It's easier than fighting it."

"They will try to define you because their minds are narrow and limited," Suzanne explains. "But once you figure out who you truly are, you will have the advantage of surprise. They won't be able to predict your moves or be able to figure you out."

"Ok, UCLA, you are growing on me!" Henry says. "I like the way you think!"

****

Suzanne and Henry are in good spirits as they trek along the road. They are confident that together they can find their way home. However, daylight is slowly fading. Soon, they will need to find shelter for the night.

"I am hungry and thirsty," Suzanne says.

"Me too," says Henry. "We need to stop and get some food and drink and find a resting place before it is dark." Suddenly, they hear a roar in the sky. They look up and see something flying overhead. It is hard to identify, but certainly is something they have never seen before.

Moreover, it is obviously menacing. It appears to be circling them. Suzanne and Henry are standing on the Yellow Brick Road staring into the sky, fixated on the unidentified flying object.

"What the fuck is that?" Henry asks in fear.

"I don't know," Suzanne responds.

"Maybe we should take cover!" Henry suggests. Before they could move, the object rapidly descends on their position. They hear a loud roar. The thing comes into view moments later. It is the flying lion with the West Witch on its back.

The lion swoops down and lands on the road about ten yards away from them. The witch nimbly jumps off his back and walks toward them. The lion begins liking himself as the witch approaches ominously.

Suzanne and Henry are stunned. They can barely move. The witch's awkward, creepy walk immobilizes them, much like a deer caught in headlights.

"So, you're the one who killed my sister," the witch declares.

"I'm so sorry," Suzanne replies empathetically. "I swear, it was an accident."

"Oh, an accident, you say! We are about to have a couple more accidents in a few moments." The Witch scowls.

"I was just a passenger on the plane......"

"Silence!" the witch commands. "Is it also an accident you are wearing my sister's ring that has been passed down through five generations of my family?"

"I-I was given this ring and told that it will protect me on my travels to see the Wizard," Suzanne mentions.

"Well, it's not your property, so give it here now, and I will spare you from a long, painful death," the witch insists.

"Don't do it, Suzanne!" Henry asserts. "If she had the power to take it, she wouldn't be asking."

"And who might you be?" the witch asks.

"You can call me Jay Z or HOVA," Henry proclaims.

"This has been a heavenly vacation thus far for you both," the witch sneers. "If I don't have that ring in my possession in a few seconds, your worst nightmares will come true!"

"She's bluffing!" Henry declares. The witch's face turns to an angry snarl.

"I have run out of patience with the two of you!" she cries. Maura spreads her arms out wide, palms facing up. She lowers her head and starts chanting unintelligibly. The lion roars, sending shivers through the bodies of Suzanne and Henry as they stand frozen. A low rumbling sound coming from the north intensifies by the moment.

"What the hell is that?" Henry whispers to Suzanne.

"I don't know, but it can't be good!" she says. They look out and see grass and bushes rustling in the distance, headed their way like a title wave. They focus their eyes to get a glimpse of what the disturbance might be.

"Oh, shit!" Henry screams, "Rats!" Thousands of rats are charging straight for them. "Run!" Henry shouts. Suzanne and Henry turn and run south as fast as they can. The witch swings her arms in their direction, directing the rats to attack.

"Oh, my God!" Suzanne shouts as she hops over branches and sprints through the forest. They hear thousands of short, high-pitched squeaks from aggressive rats as they are running for their lives. "Bluffing?" Suzanne says to Henry.

"How was I to know she could summon rats?" Henry emphasizes. Suzanne is just behind Henry. The rats catch up to Suzanne but do not attack her. Instead, they run past her, and a few jump on Henry and start biting him. Henry screams and flicks them away as he continues running furiously.

"Get off of him!" Suzanne screams.

A sign up ahead reads, *"The South – Welcome to Quadling Country."* More rats jump on Henry. He begins to slow down as a dozen rats are now chewing on his flesh. He falls across the sign meaning they have physically crossed into the southern territory. The rats on Harry start to catch fire and the rest quickly scurry back in the direction they came from, along with the rest of the herd.

Henry has several bite marks all over his body. Suzanne runs over to him. "Are you ok?" she asks, concerned. Henry is still on the ground.

"Yeah, I'm fine. What the fuck was that?"

"I don't know, Suzanne replies, "but they seem to have lost their power once you crossed into the south."

"Well, how bout we go this way, then," Henry proposes," pointing further south.

"I'm certainly not going back that way," Suzanne states, regarding the northern direction. "I fucking hate rats!"

"You?" Henry says. "There ain't a black person alive that likes rats!"

"I'm just glad you are ok," Suzanne says. "We need to find some food and water fast!"

Chapter 5 – Temporary Sanctuary

Speak No Evil

Daylight is fading fast. Morale is low. The incident with the rats took a lot out of them. Suzanne and Henry have been wandering aimlessly now for some time. Their mouths are dry; their bellies are empty. Hunger pains and thirst consume their minds. The loss of hope and uncertainty intensifies their growing melancholic demeanors. They are in a foreign land with no plan or idea of where to find their next drink or meal.

"What are we gonna do?" Henry asks. "We have no clue where we are going. We might die of thirst out here."

"Stay positive, Henry," Suzanne affirms. "We must be coming close to some sort of civilization soon. Gwendolyn rules this area. The people here must be nice."

"I hope you're right," Henry responds. A few seconds later, the two spot several cottages in the distance.

"Over there, look," Suzanne points out.

"There's gotta be at least some water around here for someone to have built houses," Henry says.

They approach the first cabin they come upon. The door is open. They step inside tentatively.

"Hello?" Suzanne yells out. "Is anyone here? We come in peace." No one answers.

"You smell that?" Henry asks.

"Yeah, what is it?" asks Suzanne. Henry enters the kitchen and spots a pot of water still expelling steam. They also see several burning candles.

"Whoever was cooking couldn't have gone very far," Henry proclaims.

"We should hurry then," Suzanne recommends. They look on the floor and find several wooden buckets filled with water, tantamount to a gallon each, covered by what appears to be some sort of saran-wrap substance. They both take turns chugging from it. In their haste, they spill some of it on the floor and more on their shirts. Once they had their fill, they began rummaging through the cabinets, looking for food. During their search, they hear a *metallic thud* coming from one of the bedrooms. They both freeze simultaneously, hearing the sound and looking at one another with their hands proverbially still in the cookie jar. Henry puts his index finger up to his mouth and stretches his lips outward as they remain as silent as possible. Henry picks up a sharp chef's knife from the counter and walks cautiously toward the room where he believes the sound came from. Suzanne follows close behind.

Henry slowly opens the first-floor bedroom door. There are also lit candles burning. No one appears to be in the small room, however. Suzanne nudges his right shoulder from behind.

"Check the closet!" Henry turns, a bit alarmed and slightly agitated by the surprise nudge.

"I'm gonna!" he responds anxiously. Before he takes a step further, a male with pale white skin, no eyeballs, and no mouth jumps out of the closet. He is moaning, which, sounds like he is trying to scream with a hand over his mouth. It sends shivers up their spines. The 'man' aggressively runs toward them. They both scream and run frantically for the front door. As they leap through the front door frame and back into the woods, they notice more pale mouthless people coming out of the woods to chase them. Again, they are sprinting for their lives. However, more mouthless people appear in every direction. Within seconds, they are surrounded.

They stop and stand back-to-back. A chorus of creepy moans and aggressive hand gestures send them into the final stage of hopelessness. They are surrounded!

"Well, I guess this is it," Henry Says.

"Yeah, it was great knowing you," Suzanne responds.

Seconds later, an Asian woman walks confidently through the angry mob and into the circle. She looks nothing like the others!

"Who are you!" she asks firmly. "Were you sent by the West Witch?"

"We are certainly not with the West Witch!" Suzanne confirms decisively.

"Well, who are you then, and why are you here?" the Asian woman asks.

"I am the person who killed the East Witch, and I'm trying to get back home to New Jersey!" she replies angrily. The *Skin People* immediately change their demeanor. They become curious as they look around at one another.

"You are the one who killed the East Witch?" the Asian woman responds incredulously.

"Yes!" Suzanne replies. "I didn't mean to, but it happened. And the little people gave me her ring to protect me from the West Witch, who, by the way, just sent a horde of rats after us and chased us this way. That's why we wound up here."

The Asian woman creeps closer to Suzanne. She is fixated on the ring.

"May I?" she asks. Suzanne reaches her right hand outward. The Asian woman grabs hold of it delicately and inspects the ring. "Oh, my!" she says after a brief look. The Asian woman shows the ring to one of the *Skin People,* who graciously approves with a casual head nod. The Asian woman's body language goes from very tense to mild and loose. "My name is *Kimiko Liang*. Most people are too ignorant to pronounce it, so I go by Kimmie." She extends her hand.

"I am Suzanne, and this is Henry." After shaking hands, Kimmie says, "Would you like to join us for some food and drinks? We have much to discuss."

"It would be our pleasure," Suzanne responds.

Three's Company

They all congregate back at the big cabin, which is where they hold their group functions. This cabin fits more than twenty people comfortably. As they enter, they notice several strange machines that act as *infusion pumps* for the residents in attendance. Except for Kimmie, all of the residents are mouthless. Therefore, they have devised a way to break down their foods into liquid forms and administer them intravenously via the infusion pumps. However, they were once people with mouths, so they know how to cook food for people with mouths.

Moreover, Kimmie has been a God

send to them, and they treat her as their exalted dignitary. She has a personal chef, among other comforts to keep her happy and satisfied. All cooks are on staff at this time, preparing food for their guests.

"Would you like a drink?" Kimmie asks.

"A drink?" Suzanne responds. "Like water, you mean?"

"No! Like a drink, alcohol?" Kimmie responds.

"Alcohol?" Henry says. "Ah, hell yeah! That would be great! What do you have?"

"They have these green berries out here that have some type of intoxicating liquids inside them. Kinda tastes like whiskey. They call them *Intemperance Berries*."

"Maybe this place ain't so bad after all," Henry jests.

"Tell them that," Kimmie replies sarcastically.

"What happened to their mouths?" Suzanne asks. "Were they born that way?"

"Oh, God, no!" Kimmie replies. "They are the *Oskin* people. They had mouths at one point. They were from the west. They revolted against the tyranny of the West Witch's mother, and she cursed them to be like you see them now. They fled the west to the south, where Gwendolyn promised them sanctuary, and thus, helped their species survive."

"What's the deal with the witches?" Henry asks.

"There are four witches," Kimmie explains. The *North Witch* and the *South Witch* are sisters—the third generation of the *Beaumont* family. The *East Witch* and the *West Witch* are sisters, also third generation, and from the *Thanatos* family. Their grandparents on their father's side of both families ruled somewhat peacefully over their current territories."

"Were they witches as well?" asks Suzanne.

"They were, but they all practiced *White Magic*, a very benign type of sorcery. Both families swore an oath to serve the Queen and help her rule the land. However, Jezebeth and Maura's parents grew tired of sharing the land with the Beaumont family. They had many disputes over borders, ideals, and laws. So, the Thanatos family made a decision that would change the course of history in Oz forever. They decided to learn *Dark Magic*. Some legends say they were educated and enticed into the ways of dark sorcery by a strange older man who came from the sky with advanced knowledge in many areas. No one really knows, though, and no one has seen the man. Conflict and war between the two families broke out. It is a war that still rages on today. The Thanatos family raised their two children in the dark arts. The children became very powerful, especially Maura, who is the most powerful of all the witches."

"Man!" Suzanne utters. "I really stepped in it this time!"

"Why are you not like the mouthless people?" Henry asks. "Where are you from?"

"I am from California," Kimmie says.

"You are one of us!" Suzanne shouts. "How did you get here?"

"I was on a date with my boyfriend, *Richard*," Kimmie says. "He took me on a helicopter ride around *Los Angeles*. All of a sudden, the helicopter started shaking wildly. I looked up and saw this strange hole in the sky. Next thing I knew, I was taken in by these people. That was like a month ago, as far as I can remember. They said they found me in the eastern territory, right at the southern border."

"What happened to your date?"

"I don't know," Kimmie responds. "They told me that I was the only one they found. I insisted we go back and look for him. We searched the crash site for hours, but there was no sign of him. Unfortunately, we found the pilot, who appeared to have died on impact."

"Woh! That's tragic! I am so sorry!" Henry laments.

"How do you communicate with them?" Suzanne asks.

"Surprisingly, they write in English," Kimmie tells her. "They gave me the rundown of what this place is about. I asked them every question I could think of. It's not like I had anything better to do. Now, I'm just trying to survive this new reality."

"I get it," Suzanne explains. "We are both from California as well. This place is not and never will be our home. Both the north and south witches told me the Wizard could get us home. You should come with us. You don't belong here."

"That is wishful thinking on steroids, I must say," Kimmie asserts. "How in the world can someone help us get home when no one knows how we even got her in the first place? Look around. It's not the most advanced culture. They don't even have cars here, for God's sake!"

"I don't know?!" Suzanne replies. "But they clearly have magic. it's worth a shot!"

"That sounds like a blind challenge with limited odds," Kimmie asserts. "We have a safe haven here. We can live out our days in comfort."

"This is not our home!" Suzanne declares. "What about your loved ones back home? Won't they be missing you?"

"I miss them every day!" Kimmie proclaims. "But getting killed trying to get back to them won't solve that problem."

"Sounds like you just need some *courage*," Henry interjects.

"Maybe you're right!" Kimmie states. "But I have been told what's out there. You have no idea the horrors you will face if you expose yourself to this place!"

"I am from New Jersey!" Suzanne states. "I have faced enough horrors there that have prepared me for anything. Furthermore, I need to get home to the ones I love. And anything that gets in the way of that will be fuckin sorry! Oh, and did you forget that I have the East Witch's ring?" Suzanne holds the ring up. It shines brightly. Kimmie looks at it in amazement. "The South Witch said it will protect me on my journey."

"So, you say this Wizard guy can actually get us home?" Kimmie asks.

****

The group gathers outside in the morning. Kimmie hugs several of the *Oskin* people and exchanges hand gestures with them, some sort of Oskin sign language. It is a tearful goodbye as the Oskin people have grown to love Kimmie as she did them. Kimmie brought her backpack with her that she had filled with dry foods and water carried in dead animal skins that had been stitched together for their journey. Suzanne, Henry, and Kimmie are soon walking back into the woods in search of the *Yellow Brick Road*.

On the Road Again

Suzanne, Henry, and Kimmie walk through the dense forest, searching for the brightly colored road. Because Suzanne and Henry had been running from the rats, they were not exactly sure where the road was located. After an hour of walking, doubt was starting to set in.

"We are never gonna find this road?" Kimmie announces. "Are you guys sure you know where you are going?"

"I think we need to go east a bit," Suzanne mentions.

"No, I'm certain that we traveled far south to get here. We need to travel north," Henry suggests adamantly. Because of his insistence, Suzanne and Kimmie followed his suggestion.

Witch Direction?

After more than an hour of walking, a yellow road appears.

"Look," Suzanne shouts. "It's the *Yellow Brick Road!*"

"Well, I'll be damned," Kimmie gushes.

"Good job, Henry!" Suzanne says.

"Let's get out of here, guys," Henry declares. After a few minutes of walking in silence, Suzanne decides to ask a question that has been gnawing at her for some time.

"Does anyone else think it's weird that we are all from California?"

"Yeah, I was thinking that myself," Kimmie responds.

"Maybe it has something to do with the location of Oz that we landed in," Henry surmises.

"What do you mean?" Suzanne asks.

"Well, we all arrived in the eastern section of Oz," Henry explains. "Maybe we all went through the same portal, which led to the same area."

"Hmm, that's an interesting observation," Kimmie replies.

"So, maybe there are other portals in other areas in our world that lead to different territories in Oz or even elsewhere?" Suzanne theorizes.

"That's what I was thinking," Henry agrees.

"Woh!" Kimmie shouts. "What is that?" She points to a fork in the road. The Yellow Brick Road splits off into three separate directions. Because the forest is so dense, it is impossible to see where each winding road leads.

"Oh my God, what do we do?" Kimmie asks.

"Let's ask that old lady over there," Suzanne suggests. The old lady is about twenty yards away, picking apples from a tree. She is wearing a red hooded sweatshirt and has a peculiar-looking face, appearing leathery and overly wrinkled. Her nose is distractingly big. She has olive-colored skin and a noticeably thick, dark mole by her nose, with several smaller dark moles on her face. Her back is hunched forward significantly. She looks to be in her eighties. Judging by the shape of her mouth, it appears she has no teeth.

"I don't think this is a good idea," Kimmie says.

"She must be from around here," Suzanne prognosticates. "She probably knows her way around." Suzanne walks over to the woman. Henry follows but stops a few feet behind Suzanne. Kimmie stays far back. "Excuse me miss." The old woman turns and appears surprised.

"Hello, dear," the woman responds. "You startled me."

"I'm so sorry," Suzanne says. "We are lost and trying to get to the Emerald City, ma'am. We were told that this road leads there. But it seems we must choose which direction to go, and we have no clue what to do."

"Call me *Bela*, dear, the woman says. "Oh, the apples this time of year are so tasty!" the woman declares in a brittle, croaky voice. "Would you like to try one?" Suzanne is a bit confused by the woman's response. She wasn't sure if the woman had understood her or not. She also wasn't sure if the woman sensed the desperation in her voice.

"No, thank you," Suzanne responds politely. "We just need to get to the Emerald City. It's an emergency!" The other two walk over and are now standing next to Suzanne.

"You must be very careful around here when picking apples," the old lady says. "Did you know that there is a certain type of apple, that if eaten, will taste sweet at first but can kill you? The sweet taste will quickly become a burning hot pain in your mouth and stomach. Your throat will swell, and the area around your mouth will blister and become inflamed, accompanied by severe digestive problems. Even touching the leaves briefly or using the tree as shade from the rain can cause blistering lesions on your skin that could leave permanent scars. And if you are near when it is set on fire, and the smoke gets in your eyes, it can cause permanent blindness. It must be the sick sense of humor of the Gods to have made nature so beautiful and enticing to the eye but so deadly to the touch!"

The three are thoroughly creeped out

by her short, gloomy soliloquy.

"Well, thanks for the apple education," Kimmie responds. "But it is urgent that we remain on the fastest road to the Emerald City."

"Oh, forgive me, child, for my long-winded speech," the old lady laments. "It has been some time since I have conversed with anyone. The road that leads to the Emerald City is the road to the right."

"Are you sure?" Kimmie asks.

"I have lived here for many years, dear. The road to the left will lead you to the north. The road in the center will lead you to the west. Stay on the road to the right, and you will reach the Emerald City in a few hours."

"Oh, thank you so much!" Suzanne gushes.

"Would you like a few apples for your trip?" the old woman asks as she extends her right hand and holds out an apple.

"No, no," Henry says with a wince. "We have plenty of food, but thank you for the offer."

"Thanks for your help," Suzanne says. The three walk off to the right, following her directions. The old woman watches them walk away with a sinister look on her face.

"Yo, that bitch was crazy, yo," Henry declares. "I don't think we should follow her directions!"

"We don't have much of a choice," Suzanne replies. "We can't just randomly choose a direction. Plus, she was a little off but seemed nice."

"I don't know," Kimmie responds. "She was creepy! I have a weird feeling about her!"

"Let's try right for a bit," Suzanne suggests. "If we think we are going the wrong way at some point, we can turn around at any time." Henry and Kimmie shrugged their shoulders, not sold on the idea. However, they didn't have a better option in mind.

After a thirty-minute walk, the landscape completely changes aesthetically. It was once a beautiful area. However, these three would not know this. The bright light emanating from the sun only illuminates the many deficiencies in the landscape that had undoubtedly arisen from years of animosity between the two defacto ruling families: the *Thanatos* and the *Beaumont* families, and not the technical rulers, which is the Queen of Emerald City.

The dark magic ignited by the Thanatos family, lasting by now for close to a century, has undoubtedly taken its toll on this particular area and on its inhabitants. It is as if the darkness had seeped into the land and its residents and taken on a life of its own. The once crystal clear, sparkling rivers and streams are now murky, dappled, and brackish. The leaves on the trees have lost their shine and never appear to flourish properly. A thick lingering fog suffocates the land as if it is an evil vapor emanating from the West Witch. Many of the rich fields that used to be home to an abundance of grains and vegetables have been reduced to barren, dry soil. They pass by broken fences as the land reclaimed itself due to the impoverished conditions caused by the power struggle between the witches.

"Where the hell are we?" Kimmie says.

"I don't know, but this area looks like

it came straight out of a horror movie!" Henry states.

"Let's just stay focused," Suzanne suggests. "We just need to follow the road."

Suddenly, they see a cornfield ahead with grass as high as seven-feet tall. The Yellow Brick Road leads straight through the tall grass but curves to the right up ahead. They cannot see if the road leads through the entire cornfield.

"I have a bad feeling about this!" Kimmie explains. "The *Oskins* told me a story about a cornfield inhabited by evil trolls or zombie-like creatures located in the west. They said that no one who has ever entered the field has come out alive."

"Surely, there must be several corn fields in Oz," Suzanne surmises. "This is a farming community. I don't think Gwendolyn would lead us into a zombie-infested cornfield. Plus, why would we be in the west? The Yellow Brick Road doesn't run through the west."

"I don't know," Kimmie responds.

"Something definitely seems off," Henry replies. "I think we should turn around."

"I'm not going in there, no way!" Kimmie blurts out.

"Look, we have come this far," Suzanne says. "Let's just stay close and get through this as fast as possible," Suzanne proposes. "The sun is setting, and darkness is only an hour away, so we must get through this before we are unable to see." Henry and Kimmie look at each other with unsure looks on their faces.

Chapter 6 – The Deception

The Cornfield

The Yellow Brick Road seems to lead through the cornfield. However, because it appears to curve to the right, they cannot visually confirm the continuance of the road. They walk forward cautiously. Kimmie is particularly spooked, and it shows in her body language. All of them are hypersensitive to any possible sound or movement. However, thus far, there have been no signs of trouble. After a few minutes of walking, they began to loosen up.

"See?" Suzanne boasts. "Nothing to worry about."

"Don't start patting yourself on the back just yet," Kimmie responds. "We have no idea how long this cornfield is."

"Why do I feel like something is tickling my face?" Henry asks.

Within minutes, they come upon the curve to the right. As soon as they make the turn, they realize that the Yellow Brick Road ends with no visible path through the wall of corn stovers.

"What is this?" Henry proclaims as he gestures toward the corn blockade.

"Oh, this is not good!" Suzanne states.

"That's it!" Kimmie announces. "I'm turning around!" Kimmie quickly does a one-eighty. "What the fuck? Where did the road go?" She looks and sees no Yellow Brick Road in any direction. They are in the middle of the cornfield.

"We've been tricked," Henry realizes.

"Ok, ok," Suzanne says in a panic, "let's just keep moving."

"In what direction?" Kimmie asks. "We could be in here for hours. We have no idea in what direction this ends. I should have never come with you! I had it made in that village!" Kimmie stomps her right foot hard on the ground. "Dammit!"

"I am so sorry that I led us into this mess," Suzanne laments.

"Wait, wait," Henry says. "The sun

rises in the east and sets in the west."

"Oh, great," Kimmie responds. "he's Nostradamus now!"

"The fortune-teller guy?" Suzanne asks in confusion.

"Yeah; he was also an astrologer," Kimmie responds.

"Oh, I didn't know that," Suzanne says. Henry is staring intently at the sun.

"Well, get on with it," Kimmie says to Henry.

"Well," Henry continues, "the sun is setting there," he points at it. "So, that way is west. And, if we are in the west, then we will need to run in the opposite direction of the sun to reach Emerald City. Now, we probably haven't traveled too far into the west, so we should angle slightly north as well."

"Well, that's as good of a guess as we got," Kimmie states. "We are so fucked!" She rolls her eyes.

"That's amazing, Henry!" Suzanne exclaims. Just then, they start hearing faint groaning sounds.

"What was that?" Kimmie asks anxiously.

"I don't know, but we'd better get a move on," Suzanne announces. They start walking quickly in the opposite direction of the sun, angling slightly to the left as Henry had suggested. The sun is sinking fast.

They soon come upon a scarecrow hanging high above them on a thick wooden stick. The menacing-looking scarecrow has a mask pulled over its head with a surrounding flap that ends near the shoulders. The mask is stitched together, including cross-stitching over each eye in the shape of an X. The mouth also has several stitches running vertically along and over its lips. Its build looks more like a muscular football player rather than clothes stuffed with hey.

"I'm gonna fucking have nightmares about that thing for sure," Kimmie says while looking up at the menacing figure. They continue a fast-paced walk toward what they hope is the Emerald City. A few seconds later, Bela, the old lady who gave them directions earlier, walks up to the scarecrow they had just passed. She reaches into her pocket and pulls out some type of white powder. She holds it up in her right palm and blows it onto the scarecrow. Suddenly, the scarecrow starts to move— slowly at first, but then begins to aggressively wiggle and shake. It awkwardly dislodges itself from the stick, jumps down, and stands next to Bela.

"You are free!" the old woman mutters. "Now go and bring those three to me, dead or alive!" The scarecrow cannot run very fast, but it stands about six feet five inches tall and looks like it can do some damage. Up ahead, the crew continues walking fast through the field, looking in all directions for any signs of danger. A quick rustling of the grass off to their left startles them.

"What was that?" Kimmie asks impatiently.

"I don't know, but I heard something," Suzanne says. Seconds later, they hear more rustling sounds, this time on their right.

"Something is following us," Kimmie blurts out.

"More like hunting us, I think," Henry replies.

Minutes later, they hear major

rustling behind them. Whatever is there is approaching fast. They stop and turn around and wait anxiously. Moments later, the scarecrow emerges. It stares at them while standing motionless.

"Hi, are you hear to help us get out of here?" Suzanne asks reluctantly. The scarecrow just stands frozen.

"What do we do?" Kimmie asks nervously as she slowly takes a few steps backward.

"We are just trying to get to the Wizard," Henry says. "Can you help us?" The scarecrow just stares at him with absent eyes. Unexpectedly, it aggressively charges toward them. Kimmy screams! All three of them are frozen in shock and fear.

Before they could process the situation, the fleet-footed, agile scarecrow tackles Henry with a human spear-style takedown, lowering its head and shoulders and driving its right shoulder into Henry's ribs at high speed. The force thrusts Henry's body backward and to the ground. It takes him a second to regain his senses. Kimmie continues screaming in terror. The scarecrow straddles Henry and puts its large gloved hand over his face and mouth, trying to suffocate him. Henry fights back, swinging, punching, and trying to grab the scarecrow's face. Henry manages to flip the creature around. Suzanne rushes over and begins kicking it in the head and stomach areas.

Henry tries to hold it down and contain it to no avail. The scarecrow pushes Henry off of him, sending Henry flying through the air. The scarecrow quickly gets to its feet. Suzanne is closest to it. The monster charges and backhands her in her face with its right hand. Suzanne flies backward, flattening several corn stovers along the way, and lands temporarily unconscious. It turns its focus toward Kimmie.

"Oh shit!" she screams as she begins running away. She tries to run by the creature on its left side, but it dives outward and tackles her. During the brief tussle, the scarecrow manages to flip Kimmie onto her back and get on top of her. It straddles her and begins strangling her with both hands. Kimmie tries desperately to fight back. She grabs hold of its hands, but she struggles to break the grip. It is too strong. She gags and fights for a breath. Henry gets up and charges it. He tries to tackle it off Kimmie, but the scarecrow shrugs its shoulder sharply, and Henry goes flying. The Scarecrow proves incredibly strong. Henry gets up and charges again. He gets the scarecrow in a headlock. The scarecrow releases its grip on Kimmie's neck, giving her a moment to catch her breath inadvertently. The figure reaches back with its right arm, clutches the back of Henry's shirt, and throws him with great force, sending him flying ten feet away, where he lands on his back.

Suzanne had awoken by now. The scarecrow resumes its chokehold on Kimmie. Suzanne charges and starts ripping hey out of the back of the scarecrow. This seemed to only anger it as it swings its right hand furiously backward while still choking Kimmie with its left. It strikes Suzanne in her chest, jolting her back violently. It resumes strangling Kimmie with both hands. Her face starts turning blue. She is gasping for air as she desperately tries to fight off her attacker. She is only seconds away from losing consciousness. Suzanne jumps up, reaches into her pocket, and grabs the lighter she had accidentally lifted from her brother. She promptly picks up a corn stover and lights it on fire. She holds the fiery end onto the lower back of the scarecrow. It catches, and a low flame quickly spreads up the scarecrow's back. Kimmie's eyes start rolling upward, but the scarecrow abruptly breaks the grip when it realizes that it is on fire. The Scarecrow stands up and twirls in a panic, trying to extinguish the fire. However, it is unable to reach its back. It twists and turns frantically as the flames quickly consume it. Within a few seconds, the scarecrow is lying face down and engulfed in flames.

Kimmie is holding her neck with both hands. She gasps, chokes, and groans from the pain. Henry comes to seconds later. He looks up while lying on his back in shock as the scarecrow burns into a pile of ashes.

"You did that?" he asks Suzanne, who had rushed over to Kimmie to see if she was ok.

"Sometimes smoking cigarettes can save your life!" she promulgates as she holds up her red Bic lighter.

"Are you ok?" Henry asks Kimmie as they both kneel over her to assess the damage.

"I can't believe I followed you assholes!" she barely blurts out, trying to regain her composure. Both Suzanne and Henry chuckle.

"She's fine," he says. He grabs her hand and helps her to her feet. Kimmie's neck is still in pain. Plus, she is still trying to recover her breathing.

Before they can fully gather themselves, they hear heavy groaning sounds approaching rapidly. A bushy-dark-haired zombie troll emerges through the corn. He is bent at the knees with his buttocks nearly touching the ground. However, he springs toward them hostilely, springing up to almost eight feet off the ground at the height of his leap. The crew runs desperately, following Henry. Ten more skinny, nearly naked zombie trolls give chase. They spring forward like angry grasshoppers on steroids, foaming from their mouths.

"What the fuck!" Henry screams!

"Run!!!" Suzanne shouts.

Henry is leading that way. Suzanne is behind him. Kimmie is trailing. Kimmie is running full speed. However, she looks back several times. This slows her down. In her mind's eye, she sees herself getting caught and consumed by these strange, scary creatures. Henry finds the exit of the cornfield seconds later. He stops prior to exiting it in order to usher the females through, using himself as a shield.

"Hurry, this way!" he yells. Suzanne clears the cornfield and falls to the ground in exhaustion.

"Come on!" Henry yells to Kimmie as he sees the zombies closing in. Kimmie passes Henry and dives out of the cornfield. Henry throws a punch and an elbow, knocking one of the zombies backward. However, more rush him. He back peddles slightly, trying to clear the cornfield, but he is still within the confines. Suzanne and Kimmie gather themselves and realize that Henry is still inside. They see corn stovers rustling violently right in front of them. They hear Henry scream!

"Henry!" Suzanne shouts. However,

there is no response. Suddenly, Henry sticks his head and hand out of the cornfield.

"Help!" he cries in a panic before being violently pulled back in. Suzanne and Kimmie see a bit of rustling in the area where Henry withdrew, then there is silence.

"Henry!" Suzanne screams.

"Oh, my God, what do we do?" Kimmie asks nervously. Suzanne starts to cry.

"I don't know," Suzanne says. A few tense moments of complete silence go by. The two women look on with bated breath. Henry was gone! Just before they gave up on him, Henry's head and right arm come out of the cornfield again. He is squirming and fighting frantically.

"Help me!" he screams as he reaches out his right hand. Suzanne grabs it with her right hand and holds on for dear life.

"Get me outa here!" he cries. Kimmie rushes forward and grabs Henry's arm. They both pull backward with all their might. Yet, they are having trouble gaining any ground. Moreover, Henry starts moving back into the cornfield, pulling them along with him.

They are losing the tug of war.

Further and further into the cornfield Henry goes until his head has nearly disappeared. Suzanne digs in and pulls with all her might. Just when all seemed lost, Henry springs free and into the arms of Suzanne and Kimmie. They all fall to the ground a few feet from the cornfield. The zombies growl and grunt. However, they are unable to leave the confines of the cornfield.

Their faces slowly fade back into the abyss. The three of them lay on the ground on their backs, exhausted for the moment, looking up at the sky. They are all breathing heavily and at their wit's end. Up ahead, they see a mountain that appears to be standing in the way of them and the Emerald City.

Heart of the Matter

After regaining their composure, the group notices a mountainous region up ahead. Only a small portion of the sun can be seen fading over the horizon. The peak of the mountain leads directly east. Luckily for them, they won't need to climb to the top to get to the other side. A dirt trail leads through the left side of the mountain and is less than half as high as the summit. Even though they caught a break not having to climb the steep mountain to its peak, there was still a-ways to travel to get around it. Moreover, darkness is approaching fast.

"Can we stop for a few minutes?" Kimmie asks. "These legs were not made for hiking."

"It's gonna be dark soon," Suzanne mentions. "We might as well find a spot to camp for the night.

"Maybe we can find a good spot up ahead," Henry says. "Keep your eyes open." Before they take another step, a cacophony of ear-piercing sounds comes from above.

"YAAAAAK! YAAAAAK! YAAAAAK!"

Kimmie immediately puts her hands over her ears. Suzanne looks at Henry anxiously. Henry abruptly looks up.

"Oh shit!" Henry shouts. Suzanne looks up as well.

"Is that a Pterodactyl?" Suzanne says in awe.

"A what?" Kimmie asks nervously.

"A flying reptile!" Henry says firmly.

"Squawk, squawk, squawk!"

Two more Pterodactyls come into view. They are circling the sky not far above the crew. One of them swoops down. It looks as if it is headed straight for the group. The flapping of his wings grows louder by the moment. All three of them are staring up at the wonders in the sky.

"YAAAAAK! YAAAAAK! YAAAAAK!"

"Ah, I think we should RUN!" Henry exclaims. Kimmie screams as her feet shuffle. The screaming reptile breaks out of his dive and swoops by the group, barely missing Suzanne's head with his sharp feet, which provide the same amount of force as an alligator's bite!

"Whoosh, whoosh, whoosh," the sound of the large wings flapping as the reptile recedes back into the sky, covering the remaining sunlight for a few moments as it ascends. Suzanne, Henry, and Kimmie run with all their might, looking for a place to hide, stopping only momentarily to dodge the incoming Pterodactyls. They are exhausted, but their survival instincts have overwhelmed their senses. One by one, the

Pterodactyls continue to swoop down to a chorus of unpleasant retile noises. It is as if they are setting up to take one of the running humans. One of them catches Kimmie on her arm with his claw-like feet in a failed attempt to snatch her up.

"Ouch!" Kimmie cries out. The claw only manages to graze her shoulder, but still rips through her shirt and mildly tears through her skin. The blow knocks her off her feet. Henry stops and rushes over to her. Suzanne, who is trailing behind, rushes over to her as well. Both Henry and Suzanne quickly help Kimmie to her feet and drag her toward cover. The next Pterodactyl swoops down. This time, it manages to clutch onto Suzanne's shirt. It lifts her off of the ground. She screams in terror as the flying reptile ascends. Another beast swoops past Suzanne's face while chomping its beak as if trying to take a bite of her.

BANG!

A gun blast sounds and a muzzle flashes brightly from nearby. Suzanne falls from the dark sky, hitting the ground hard just off the trail. She is unconscious. The blast hits the Pterodactyl and, after releasing Suzanne, falls to the ground on its long, birdlike beak further down the mountain and out of sight. Kimmie and Henry look over and see a man in *U.S. Army fatigues* holding an AR15. Henry and Kimmie quickly run over to Suzanne to check on her condition.

"Suzanne!" Kimmie says as she gently shakes her arm. "Suzanne! Are you ok?" Suzanne opens her eyes and is a bit dazed. The other two Pterodactyls are still circling above. They are even more agitated now that one of their own has been shot down.

"Guys!" the military man shouts. "This way, hurry!" They help Suzanne to her feet. Henry picks Suzanne up in a fireman's carry, and rushes toward the military man. He leads them just around the bend to a cave entrance on the side of the mountain.

****

An assortment of well-placed sticks on the cave floor holds a fire that illuminates the hollowed-out area nicely. Henry carefully places Suzanne on the ground comfortably on her back. Kimmie warms her hands over the fire.

"It can get pretty cold in this place at night, so try and stay warm," the military man suggests.

"Nice little spot ya got here, soldier," Kimmie says. "What's your name?"

"I'm *Lorenzo Rodriguez* from New Jersey. I presume you all are not from around here either."

"We are all from the U.S.," Henry responds. "I'm Henry, and that's Suzanne. We are both students at UCLA. And this is Kimmie."

"How long have you been here?" Suzanne asks.

"About two months," Lorenzo replies. "A crew of four of us were sent on a military operation. We took a *Black Hawk* for the mission. Just before we reached our destination, we started experiencing severe turbulence. We all must have blacked out cause the next thing we knew, we had crashed here. Our chopper was inoperable, and we had no idea how we had gotten here."

"Where are the others?" Kimmie asks.

"We got separated about a month ago. I went to grab some firewood just before sunset one night. I started hearing strange noises, like some strange clanking noises. All of a sudden, I found myself tussling with this metal robot or something; mean fucker. I just remember it had some cold red eyes like it was possessed. I got away, but it chased me. That thing was relentless. I got lost. When I finally went back to the campsite a day or so later, the crew had left. We didn't stay in one place for very long. There is some crazy shit out here, and most of it wants us dead."

"We noticed," says Henry.

"Honestly, I've always felt I was better off on my own anyhow," Lorenzo admits. "I've never been much of a team player, and I'm not the most empathetic person. I always say, 'Ya gotta look out for number one.' My friends say I am *heartless*. I tend to agree."

"I've only been here a couple of days," Suzanne mentions. "When my plane crashed, I met two good witches, and they told me that I needed to go to the Emerald City to see the Wizard. They said that he can get me home."

"So, we are all on a journey to see the Wizard in hopes he can get us out of this nightmare," Kimmy interjects.

"Well, sounds like a plane to me!" Lorenzo agrees. "Count me in. But we will need to wait until morning. We can't be traveling out there at nighttime."

"That's fine by me," Kimmie affirms. "I could use a good night's sleep." Lorenzo had figured out that a specific type of berry (the *Intemperance Berry,* as the mouthless people called it) held the same properties as alcohol. He had figured out a way to collect several gallons of it and stayed drunk much of each day. The crew stayed up most of the night drinking and talking about the comforts they missed from home.

****

It's morning in Oz.

Burble, burble, burble.

A boiling cauldron is sitting in a candle-lit cave on top of what looks like a stage, with stairs carved from rock leading to a higher, flat surface area. The water ripples and bubbles as it boils on high heat. There are several small cages, each filled with an important captive, all of which are impoverished, unkept, and dying from lack of care. There are tiny people in some. Others hold sky people. Some even imprison indigenous dissidents of the witch's rule. Human skeleton heads, animal body parts, and dozens of lit candles complete the décor. This is the main ritual room in the *West Witch's Liar*. It is where she spends most of her time. An attractive blonde woman hangs naked by a rope bound to her wrists and attached to the ceiling of the cave. Her feet are three-feet off the ground. One of the guards walks into the room cautiously.

"I have news, your majesty," he announces before fully committing to the room.

"You may enter," the witch replies. "What is it?"

"It has been reported that a pterodactyl was shot down in the *Crest Mountain* province. We believe that the woman with the ring is among the rebels."

"Good work!" the witch replies.

"Send in the Tin Soldier." Moments later, the tin monster enters the room. "I want this meddling little turd, and her friends squashed like bugs; you hear me! They are headed for the Emerald City. Cut them off and bring me that ring!" The Tin Soldier turns robotically, with its ax firmly at its side, and leaves the room walking with purpose. "Now, where were we," the witch says to the woman hanging as she holds a scorching hot poker to her buttocks. The woman screams in agony as the extreme heat burns and blisters her skin. The witch has branded her with '*the mark of the witch.*'

"Please, please!" the woman cries. "My sister will do your bidding!"

"Oh, she better, or you will face an unimaginable fate!" The lion is chained up nearby. The witch strolls past several cages, each with one tiny person imprisoned within. They tremble with fear as the witch approaches. Some are shaking so violently that their cages are rattling. As the witch slowly walks by each cage, she uses her long nails and scratches the metal bars of several cages, taunting the little people with the eerie metallic scraping sounds.

"*This one!*" the witch announces as she points to the unlucky soul. Two guards open the cage and drag the unwilling little person from it. They drag her kicking and screaming over to the lion, *Gedeon,* and throw her his way. Crunching sounds fill the room. The other terrified prisoners wince and look away. The woman hanging closes her eyes in terror and tries to turn her head away, so she does not witness the gruesome carnage occurring just a few feet in front of her!

****

Back at the temporary shelter, Suzanne is the first to awake. The fire had burnt out hours ago. The first light of the sun was now glaring through the cave entrance. One by one, they awoke. Everyone is hungry and thirsty. Morale is low. Everyone appears unmotivated. Not only are they suffering from physical deficiencies, but things have also taken a toll on them emotionally. However, Suzanne remains hopeful. In fact, she is excited that they are so close to the Emerald City. She believes in her heart they will all make it there and that the Wizard will help them return home.

"How far is it to the Emerald City?" Suzanne asks as everyone is getting themselves ready to leave.

"If the Emerald City is what I think it is, it's probably about an hour or so walk from here," Lorenzo explains.

"Listen," Suzanne announces firmly, "I know this is not an ideal situation for any of us! None of us asked for this shit! But here we are. And, we are in this together! If we have any hope of getting home, we need to work together to get to the Wizard. And all of us will get there, so let's remain positive. And if anything gets in our way, let's FUBAR that shit!" The inspired group remains silent. Kimmie whispers to Henry, "What's FUBAR mean?"

"Fucked up beyond all recognition," he answers.

"I do feel a bit safer with a military man with a gun," Kimmie declares.

"Let's get this show on the road," Henry proposes.

"Follow me, and keep your eyes peeled!" Lorenzo emphasizes.

****

After only a few minutes, Suzzanne and her crew reach the sub-peak of the mountain. Immediately, they can see a magnificently constructed city up ahead.

"It looks like a classier *Las Vegas* from a distance," Henry says. There was no doubt that the Emerald City is up ahead. Lorenzo uses his binoculars to take a look.

"May I see those?" Suzanne asks. She looks and spots the *Yellow Brick Road* in the distance about five hundred yards up ahead, just past a very small village filled with shacks and campsites. "Over there!" she points while still looking through the scope. "It's the yellow road!"

"Where? Let me see!" Henry says as he takes hold of the binoculars, stands firmly, and takes a look. "Well, I'll be damned. There it is."

Chapter 7 – The Emerald City

Ghost Town

The four new friends walk down the mountain heading for the castle. They must walk the dirt roads through a small village filled with small shacks. The towering castle is off in the distance but remains in sight as they walk through the village that offers no structure high enough to block the towering view of the castle. The small town appears to be abandoned. The small shacks appear severely dilapidated. Several display broken windows, many roofs have holes and gaps, and others exhibit a cracked and fissured appearance.

The quiet is disturbed when a metallic thud sounds a few feet in front of them. The *Tin Soldier* had leaped from a rooftop of a shack and landed in front of them. It lands on its right knee with its right fist on the ground, its head down, and a blood-stained ax in its left hand. The creature raises its head slowly and stands to its feet. The group is in shock. It is between them and the city.

Lorenzo is a tad-bit slow raising his weapon. Although he is a seasoned military veteran, he was not trained for combat against a non-human entity. As soon as he raised his gun and fired it, the Tin Soldier had already turned to its right and had broken into a full sprint. Lorenzo's first shot hit it in its left side, center mass. However, what would have dropped any human did not even phase the Tin Soldier. This confused Lorenzo, and he could only hit it with one more shot before the Tin Soldier disappeared into the shack with no front door.

"You got him!" Henry exclaims.

"That's the thing that was chasing me and got me separated from my team," Lorenzo mentions.

"Let's get out of here before he comes back!" Suzanne says.

"You guys go ahead," Lorenzo orders. "I have a bone to pick with that metal douche bag."

"We are not going anywhere without you!" Suzanne says firmly.

"I will catch up with you all after I reduce this thing to spare parts," Lorenzo says. "Get going!"

"He is the only one that has a weapon," Kimmie says regarding Lorenzo.

"We all need to stick together!" Suzanne suggests.

"We don't even know what that thing is," Henry confirms. "Maybe we should just keep moving."

"I shot it, and it ran," Lorenzo says confidently. "With this gun I can tear it to pieces. Plus, he will hunt us down before we even get close to that castle. Now, you guys need to leave right now! I'm not gonna say it again!"

"You heard him," Kimmie pronounces.

"Are you sure about this?" Henry asks.

"Go, NOW!" he shouts as he cautiously approaches the shack that the Tin Soldier had entered with his gun in the ready position. Suzanne is reluctant to leave, but Henry puts his hand on her shoulder and firmly suggests they get going. They all watch Lorenzo slowly approaching the shack.

"That Lorenzo's got *heart*," Henry says. "You gotta give him that." They all look at each other, unsure of what to do. "We should hurry!" Henry shouts. None of them were optimistic that Lorenzo was going to survive the showdown. Furthermore, they knew that if the Tin Soldier made quick work of Lorenzo, it would likely get to them before they reached the castle. It was time to move!

****

As the other three ran toward the castle, Lorenzo put his back to the wall next to the doorway where the Tin Soldier had run into. He peeks inside quickly and then returns to his position. It is too dark to see inside as he looks through the doorway. However, Lorenzo's rifle has a light above the barrel. He rushes inside the small cottage-style structure and vacillates his rifle in anticipation of any movement.

"Come on out, asshole!" Lorenzo

shouts. "You can't hide!" He advances cautiously into the kitchen area on high alert. "After I kill you, I'm gonna keep a piece of you as a souvenir." Lorenzo secures the living room and the kitchen. Just then, he hears a *clanking* sound coming from one of the two bedrooms down the hall. He immediately reacts and turns his attention toward that area. He is confident that he will get the best of the Tin Soldier. Not only does he have years of experience in battle, but he is fighting with an AR15 versus an ax. He believes that a shot between its eyes should short circuit the machine and shut it down. He is even cocky in anticipation of the confrontation.

He walks cautiously down the narrow hallway. At the end of it, there is a bedroom on the left, a bedroom on the right, and a bathroom straight ahead. Lorenzo anticipates that the noise came from the bedroom on his right. Lorenzo opens the door swiftly and quickly scans the room. However, he finds nothing. As he turns around, an ax strikes his gun, causing Lorenzo to drop the rifle inadvertently. The Tin Soldier grabs Lorenzo's neck with its left hand and clutches it tightly. Lorenzo uses both hands to try and loosen the grip, to no avail. The Tin Soldier tosses him down the hallway like a rag doll.

Lorenzo's back hits the ground hard and he slides a few feet. A few small pieces of wood from the floor splinter into his back. He winces and groans in pain. The Tin Soldier aggressively charges him, looking to finish him off. As it approaches, the Tin Soldier raises the ax above its head and brings it down with great force! Lorenzo somehow manages to roll to his right, avoiding the blow. The ax strikes the wooden floor, digging deep into it. As the Tin Soldier yanks the ax from the floor, Lorenzo manages to scamper behind it toward his rifle on his hands and knees. Lorenzo sees the light emanating from the rifle as he leaps from his hands and knees and grabs hold of it. The Tin Soldier forcefully yanks its ax from the floor and turns quickly. Lorenzo grabs hold of his weapon simultaneously. The Tin Soldier grabs the ax handle with both hands, raises it above its head, and flings it toward Lorenzo. At the same time, Lorenzo clutches the rifle, turns, sits up slightly, and fires a shot.

THUMP!

The spinning ax strikes Lorenzo, leaving half of the blade sticking out of his chest. Lorenzo drops the rifle inadvertently and begins convulsing and gasping for air. Lorenzo had hit the Tin Soldier with his shot. However, it had only managed to strike its *left knee*, the one it just had repaired from its battle with Mariette. The Tin Soldier limps over to Lorenzo's fatally injured body. Lorenzo tries desperately to reach for his rifle while on his back, which is only a few inches away. However, his body is no longer cooperating with his mind. His efforts are futile. The Tin Soldier finally reaches Lorenzo's frayed body. Lorenzo is gasping, groaning, and choking up blood. The Tin Soldier stands over him for a moment and stares ominously into his eyes. It turns its head sideways slightly.

"Go ahead; you fucking garbage can," Lorenzo barely blurts out. "Finish it!" The Tin Soldier raises the ax above its head and brings it down with great force! Lorenzo fades to black. The Tin Soldier cuts his head off and carries it out the door while limping.

****

The group had been running furiously toward the castle for fifteen minutes by now. Once they had cleared the small village, they came upon a swamp. Beyond the swamp is the Emerald City. Most of it is dry land. However, they would need to travel through a bit of marshland to officially enter Emerald City. They only had about a five-minute slog through waist-high water to get to dry land.

"I'm not going in there?" Kimmie exclaims regarding the sludgy water crossing.

"Kimmie, we don't need to go far in order to get to the other side," Suzanne mentioned, trying to ease her mind.

"I'm sure we can walk a bit sideways and find another way across," Kimmie suggests.

"She may be right, Suzanne," Henry asserts. "We don't know what is in these waters. And, how many times are we gonna be surprised by the multitude of alien creatures until we realize that we are not in our home anymore?"

"Look," Suzanne says firmly, "we have no clue how far behind us that psychotic robot is. For all we know, it could be close. This looks like an easy way across. I say we do it quickly and get to the castle. This is our last obstacle."

"Ok," Kimmie says, "but you go first."

"I got this!" Suzanne avows.

Suzanne takes a few steps forward. After her third step, she sinks quickly into waist-high, muddy water. The other two watch intently as she continues across. Within a couple of minutes or so, Suzanne reaches the other side. She turns and says, "See, it's fine!" Henry is next. He takes a step forward, and immediately water floods his ankles. Suddenly, a creature resembling an alligator with a shark's fin enters the water from the south-east side. Unaware of the visitor, Henry high-steps through the thick, muddy water and quickly reaches the other side.

"Come on, Kimmie," Henry shouts. "It's a piece of cake."

"Oh, what the fuck!" Kimmie says as

she starts running forward. Step after step, she moves across the muddy water until her foot gets stuck in the mud below the surface about halfway across the channel. She pulls her left leg several times but it won't budge.

"I'm stuck!" she screams.

"Don't worry," Henry replies. "I am coming."

Suzanne is looking around for the Tin Soldier or any other threats in the area. Suddenly, she spots a fin sticking out of the water moving rapidly toward Kimmie. Henry rushes back to help Kimmie.

"What the fuck is that!" Suzanne screams as she points at it.

"Oh my God!" Kimmie screams in terror. "Please get me out of here!"

Henry sprints as fast as he can through the muddy water to try and reach her. Panic ensues as the fin is getting dangerously close to Kimmie. When Henry finally reaches her, he dives underwater and yanks on her left leg. However, it won't budge. Meanwhile, the gator-shark is only seconds away from striking distance. Henry pulls and pulls her leg. Both Kimmie and

Suzanne are screaming manically. Suzanne is nervously watching the gator-shark's fin creep closer and closer to them. She calls out and warns them it's getting close, which doesn't help to keep Kimmie calm at all. Suddenly, two more gator-sharks appear, coming from the north-east side and join the hunt. One final yank from Henry releases Kimmie's leg from the mud. Kimmie makes a mad dash toward Suzanne. Henry surfaces quickly and follows close behind.

Suzanne reaches out, grabs Kimmie's hand, and pulls her to safety. Henry turns and sees all three fins only a few feet away and closing fast on his left and right. He dives forward and reaches the edge. The closest gator-shark surfaces and lunges toward Henry's feet, looking to grab hold with its razor-sharp teeth, but narrowly misses.

"Piece of cake, huh?" Kimmie says sarcastically. They are all dirty and covered in mud. Henry is on his back, breathing heavily once again.

Because they are on raised land, the group can see the Yellow Brick Road ahead.

Muddied, bloodied, battered, and bruised, the group's spirits have just risen to new heights as safety was only moments away.

****

After shifting between a full sprint and a lazy jog, the crew needs a break. They are exhausted. It didn't help that they were looking over their shoulders every few moments waiting for the Tin Soldier to appear.

"How much further do we need to go?" Kimmie asks as she tries to catch her breath. She was just being choleric and insolent, of course, because she knew that the other two did not have the answer to that question.

"I don't know," Suzanne responds. "But look over there!" She points to the Yellow Brick Road. They had found it. All they needed to do at this point is follow it straight to the castle.

The Castle

Less than a half-hour later, they arrive at the enchanting castle. It is a spectacular sight to behold. The regal structure is enormous, occupying approximately two *New York City* blocks in length and a city block in width. It is a soaring edifice with one-hundred-and-fifty rooms, bountiful gardens, and three towering turrets. Three guards armed with rifles manned the front entrance. Several more guards are on patrol at the top of the wall. They all keep in touch via a complex communication system consisting of discreet remote inductive earpieces. As the group nears the castle, two of the guards quickly approach them.

"What is your business here?" *guard-one* asks.

"We are here to see the Wizard," Suzanne replies.

"He is not taking visitors today," *guard-two* responds.

"But I am Suzanne. I have been sent

here by Zuri and Gwendolyn, the north and south witches. I killed the East Witch, by accident, of course." The two guards look at each other, a bit puzzled.

"We heard about that," guard-one says, "but how do we know that you are the one who killed her?"

"I wear the East Witch's ring," Suzanne holds out her hand. The guards are in shock.

"Wait here!" guard-two says. They walk back toward the castle's front entrance. Guard-one appears to be talking to someone on his earpiece while holding his left index finger to his left ear.

"They are never gonna let us in," Kimmie says. "This was a bad idea. They will probably arrest us and throw us in the dungeon."

"Now, why would they do that, Kimmie?" Henry asks as he rolls his eyes.

"No one in power likes to deal with common folk like us," Kimmie explains. "They might be worse than the West Witch, just a different type of power-hungry."

"Ok, let's just remain calm and trust in the process," Suzanne interrupts. "I have a lot of pull here."

"Oh, now you are a celebrity?" Kimmie asks facetiously. "Great, we have Nostradamus and Kim Kardashian. This is certainly a recipe for success," Kimmie rolls her eyes. Seconds later, guard-one and guard-two walk back over to the group.

"The Wizard will see you now," guard-one says.

"Follow us," says guard-two. Suzanne shoots a sarcastic smile at Kimmie and quickly bats her eyelashes.

Once inside the large front doors of the castle, the group is frisked by another set of guards to ensure they are not in possession of any weapons.

****

The three are escorted into a lavish waiting area that clearly has a distinctive flower theme. Not only are there several fresh flowers throughout the room, but there are also many brilliant frescos of flowers hanging on the walls. The group is exhausted. They all sit on one of the many chairs and couches in the room. After about ten minutes, Kimmie gets antsy. The group is irritable and exhausted.

"Oh, man; I'm not feeling good about this!" Kimmie says anxiously.

"What is your problem now?" Henry asks.

"They are making us wait," Kimmie responds. "That is not a good sign."

"Kimmie, there are a million reasons why the Wizard may not be ready," Suzanne mentions. "We showed up unannounced."

"She would be skeptical even if they rolled out the red carpet for us," Henry says sarcastically. Just then, a woman walks in. The group is taken aback because the woman has two noses.

"Greetings, I am *Maree*," she says. "The Wizard is excited to meet the sorcerous who slayed the East Witch and wears her ring! Come with me, please."

"I wouldn't say 'slayed' exactly, but ok," Suzanne mentions. The group follows her down a long corridor.

"I bet she 'nose' everything that goes on around here," Kimmie whispers sarcastically as she points to her own nose.

Henry tries not to laugh but can't help himself.

"That's not funny, Kimmie," Suzanne says. "Have some respect."

"It was kinda funny," Henry whispers. Suzanne rolls her eyes. Henry and Kimmie share a devious smirk. "Who 'nose' where she is taking us," Henry whispers to Kimmie, whose cheeks puff out as she tries to hold in the laughter. She takes a deep breath and composes herself. "If I find a woman with three breasts up in here, I'm marrying her," Henry says softly to Kimmie, who bursts out in laughter this time. Everyone, including the guards lining the hallway, looks at her awkwardly. She catches herself and quickly restrains her glee.

"Sorry," she says, slightly embarrassed as she flashes a clumsy smile. Thankfully, Maree was unaware of the conversation.

Maree brings them into a lavish room where dozens of dignitaries stop what they are doing and begin clapping and cheering.

"What are they doing?" Suzanne asks.

"They are cheering for you," Marlee

says. "You killed the East Witch! When we were told you were on your way, we put together a banquet in your honor."

Several maids wearing matching long black dresses with white collars and front aprons with ruffles on them can be seen all around the room. Several maintenance robots, or MRs, also assist with many of the preparation duties.

"The Queen assumed that you would be hungry after your long journey and prepared a great meal and celebration for you," Maree informs them. "Please help yourselves. The Queen will arrive shortly."

"Thank you!" they all reply kindly as their eyes bulge from their heads when they see the assortments of foods on the tables. Suzanne heads straight for the buffet. However, Henry and Kimmie see something much more tantalizing: a full bar!

They rush over to it. They see several bottles, none of which they have ever seen or heard of. However, they do recognize several complimentary drinks, such as orange juice, soda water, cranberry juice, etc. Henry grabs a bottle of clear alcohol.

He opens the cap and smells it.

"Mm, smells like vodka," he says as he holds it up to Kimmie's nose. She nods her head in agreement.

"What's that?" she asks as she points to a bottle. Henry picks it up, opens the cap, and smells it.

"That smells like tequila," he says. He puts it up to Kimmie's nose. She responds with an agreeable gesture. He picks up another bottle and does the same. This one is similar to whiskey; they both agree.

"I used to be a bartender," Henry proclaims. "I can make us a few drinks from this collection of beverages." Henry mixes a Tequila Sunrise for both of them.

"Cheers to getting home and to my new homies," Kimmie says, and they touch glasses and drink. Before long, their curiosity got the best of them, and they wanted to try something that they were not familiar with.

"What is that one?" Kimmie asks, pointing to the bottle filled with blue liquid. Henry grabs the bottle.

"It's called *Blitzky*," he announces.

"Blitzsky?" Kimmie asks. "What the

hell is that?"

Henry brings the bottle closer to his face and reads the small print on the label, *"Warning: May cause extreme euphoria and reality may become distorted."*

"Extreme euphoria???" Kimmie shouts excitedly. She snatches the bottle from Henry's hands.

"This might be a bad idea," Henry suggests.

"Has anything thus far been a good idea?" Kimmie asks rhetorically. "Plus, the best idea I've had so far is to feel euphoria," she says, ignoring the rest of the warning on the bottle. Kimmie pours three shots into a glass filled with ice and chugs it down in seconds.

"How do you feel?" Henry asks.

"I'm good," Kimmie announces. "It tastes sweet. No biggie."

"We should grab something to eat also," Henry suggests. "The food smells amazing." They reconvene with Suzanne, who has a full plate of food in hand. The buffet is lavish, including a diverse mix of good eats. Henry and Kimmie each grab a plate and dig in. The three are sitting at a nearby table eating and enjoying the first bit of comfort and security they've had in some time.

"This food is delicious!" Suzanne expresses.

"We really needed a good meal like this," Henry replies.

"My tastebuds are orgasming right now," Kimmie mentions. The look on her face is odd, like she is on heroin or something. "Food is so important," she proclaims. "Every bite is like you are chewing a piece of heaven. Oh my God, it is so beautiful." Suzanne looks at Henry with a confused look on her face.

"Kimmie, are you ok?" Suzanne asks, concerned.

"I am fabulous," Kimmie replies. "This is heaven. When is Jesus arriving?"

"What did you do to her?" Suzanne asks Henry.

"She drank some strange drink that I told her not to," Henry explains. "This is gonna be bad! We need to hide her in the closet or something."

"Oh, great!" Suzanne says frustratingly. "This is your mess! You keep her under control!"

"Do you guys see these marble floors?" Kimmie asks in wonderment. "How much do you think they cost? I bet the queen has a Ferrari and drives around town giving the finger to the West Witch, like, Bitch, you see my castle? She has no idea!"

"Oh, damn, we are fucked!" Suzanne says.

The Queen of Oz

Suzanne, her crew, and the other guests are enjoying the celebration when, unexpectedly, trumpets begin blaring from the lavish staircase, playing a bluesy, seductive groove. They all stop eating and turn toward the stairs, which lead up one level before splitting into different directions, one to the left and one to the right, both leading to another set of stairs.

A quintet of horn players is lined up uniformly on each side of the stairs. Within a few moments, the queen saunters in between them in royal fashion, appearing oblivious to her over-the-top introduction. She is wearing a beautiful long pink dress puffed out wide at the bottom with mesh sleeves and a dainty crown on her head. Her elegance is unmatched and can be seen immediately by every onlooker. The crew abruptly stops eating and stands at attention, along with everyone else. As the queen reaches the bottom of the stairs, the music stops brusquely.

"Bow!" Suzanne says to her friends nervously as she falls to one knee and bows her head. Henry and Kimmie follow suit.

"Rise!" the queen says as she raises her right hand, palm facing upward. She approaches them slowly. The three stand and face her. "I am *Queen Umaa*, ruler of Oz. I have heard much about the one who killed the East Witch. But I have many questions for you." Suzanne's mouth is dry from nerves. She gulps and nods tensely at the queen.

"It would be my pleasure, your highness," she responds. Kimmie is having a tough time keeping it together. She is looking around and daydreaming, not acknowledging the queen's presence. Suzanne and Henry are trying not to bring attention to Kimmie's mental state, but they continue to keep a close eye on her.

"Can I see it?" the queen asks.

"See it?" Suzanne responds in confusion.

"The East Witch's ring," the queen answers.

"Of course!" she says. Suzanne extends her ring hand toward the queen and bows her head. The queen clutches her hand softly and looks closely at the ring.

"Ah, yes, this is it, alright," the queen says, pleased. "This possesses great power in this land. It couldn't be on a better person's hand."

"Why, thank you," Suzanne says. "Gwendolyn said it would protect me from the West Witch."

"And indeed, it will," the queen replies. "It has protected you all." The queen starts walking. The group follows. Suzanne is walking step by step with the queen. Henry and Kimmie are a few steps behind. "Zuri and Gwendolyn have been great allies of ours. If not for them, the East and West Witch's treachery would have surely consumed the land completely by now." The queen looks at Kimmie. "Is your friend all right?" she asks. Kimmie appears to be having a staring contest with one of the queen's guards.

"We apologize, your graciousness," Henry responds. "It seems she accidentally drank some *Blitzy*."

"Oh, boy," the queen says as she chuckles. Several of the guards titter as well. "She should be ok in a few hours."

"Have you been informed that we have been sent here to see the Wizard?" Suzanne asks. "Zuri and Gwendolyn suggested we travel here to see him about possibly getting home."

"Yes, yes, the Wizard. Now, if we can only track him down. A mysterious one that Wizard is. He seems to spend a lot of time in his lab in the underneath area of the castle. No one has ever been in the lab, but his most trusted advisor, *Barkley*, who brings some of the Wizard's new inventions up from there from time to time. Barkley is the only one who has ever actually seen the Wizard. He said if he is seen, his magic could vanish. Furthermore, the West Witch has put many bounties on his head. He believes that his anonymity keeps him safe.

The Wizard believes there to be spies among us."

"Spies?" Suzanne asks.

"Yes, working for the West Witch, or so he believes."

"Oh, well, that's not good," Suzanne replies.

"The Wizard was, after all, one of the two *Sky People* prophesized to help us win this war against the evil witches."

"Who is the other?" Suzanne asks.

"Well, you, of course, my dear!" the queen responds. Suzanne has a look of shock and confusion on her face. The queen turns to one of her guards. "Go and fetch Barkley," she commands. The guard departs. "In the meantime, please enjoy some food and drink we have prepared for you! Continue the feast!" the queen announces. The music starts playing, and everyone resumes movement. The queen gracefully exits the room.

Henry grabs hold of Kimmie's arm, and they all head over to the extravagant buffet table.

"You need to eat something," Henry says to Kimmie. She looks at the food. She sees a chicken standing up in a pan.

"So, you are gonna eat me, huh?" the chicken says. Kimmie's face sinks, and her eyes bulge. "Do I not have feelings? You think I didn't have a family? Why is it ok to eat me?"

"Who?" Kimmie shouts as she turns away. "I'm not eating him! He has a family!" Henry turns to a couple of guards.

"Can you see to it that she is safely escorted to her room and doesn't come out, please?" The guards carry Kimmie off. She goes with them willingly as she is unaware of what is happening.

Intellectual Bonding

Henry goes up to the buffet for seconds. After they had their fill, they sat silently for a few moments, thinking about their situation. They have come so far but will not be satisfied until they complete the mission. The people and the comforts of home are becoming increasingly harder to put out of their minds.

"Do you really think the Wizard can help us get home?" Henry asks as he puts some stuffed blue olives onto his plate.

"I sure hope so," Suzanne responds. Both of them seem to be in pretty good spirits despite the circumstances. Henry sneezes as he is filling his plate. He puts his face in his forearm during the sneeze.

"God bless you," Suzanne says.

"Thank you," Henry responds. "Do you know why people say 'God Bless you' when someone sneezes?" Henry asks.

"No, I was just taught to say it; why?" Suzanne replies. The question puts her in a strange space mentally. She briefly wonders why she has never pondered that question.

"Well, I notice that most people regurgitate the things that they have heard or been taught without ever thinking about challenging or analyzing these things," Henry says. He is deep in thought as he puts a sausage on his plate.

"Interesting," Suzanne says. "So, why do people say it?"

"Well, back in the fourteenth century, during the *Black Death* plague, people believed that when you sneezed, your soul was expelled from your body, and, to protect against this, people said 'God bless you' to stop the devil from snatching your soul."

"Are you serious?" Suzanne asks.

"I know, it sounds crazy," Henry asserts. "I think I have sneezed like at least a thousand times by myself, and the devil hasn't snatched my soul just yet." They both laugh. "The problem is that most people believe what they have been taught is truth, and conditioned responses are hard to break. Even knowing the origin of the response is not what you expected will likely not get you to change your response. People usually defend against conflicting beliefs, even after learning that their responses are irrational."

"Wow, that is very insightful, Henry! I love the way you think!"

"I know a lot of useless information," Henry states.

"That is the furthest thing from useless information," Suzanne declares. "Just because most people don't understand it doesn't mean it is not the truth. As Shakespeare said, 'truth is truth for evermore.' That means what was true yesterday is true today and will be true tomorrow, regardless of how it is perceived by the masses today. They thought that beating and sexually harassing women was acceptable a while back because the majority accepted it. The masses believed that slavery of human beings was also acceptable. But the truth has remained the same. The only difference is our growing understanding of the truth."

"That is a great example," Henry agrees.

"I love when people say 'what doesn't kill you makes you stronger,'" Suzanne mentions. "Like if you smoke a pack of cigarettes a day and you die from getting hit by a truck, did the cigarettes help you run up the stairs faster or make you stronger?" They both laugh.

"What about when they say 'the definition of insanity is doing the same thing over and over again and expecting different results?'" Henry asks. "If you bench-press every day, aren't you going to get stronger? Doesn't practice make perfect?"

"Exactly," Suzanne agrees. "Anything I do over and over will yield different results, for better or worse. But the socially presumed meaning of the word as it is promoted is inherently wrong."

"If I ask nine women out on a date the same way and they all say no, then I ask the tenth woman, and she says yes, am I insane?" Henry raises both hands, palms facing upward, shrugs his shoulders, and crinkles the right side of his lips upward, suggesting disagreement.

"That is a good one," Suzanne says. They both laugh. They are both genuinely enjoying this connection they have with one another.

"You know what the actual definition of insanity is?" Henry asks.

"No, what, tell me?" she replies.

"Severely mentally ill," Henry explains. "Critical thinking seems to be a thing of the past."

"Well, I guess we can just let the world continue being delusional and just yes them to death," Suzanne affirms. "No use in fighting these battles. We will just drive ourselves crazy and appear pompous. You know what they say? People are more concerned with order than justice. But I am so glad that I met you, and I hope when we get through this, that we never lose touch. Because I cannot imagine not having you in my life." The two are staring at each other. The chemistry is palpable. That discussion had cemented the fact that they were both on the same page. They were both on the same mental level, and they both felt it deeply. Their eyes are locked onto one another, and they are both swept up in the movement. Just then, Maree approaches them.

"The Wizard is ready for you now," she says. "Follow me." The two break out of their hypnotic gaze and regain focus on the task at hand.

More Hoops

The inside of the castle is like a small town. Walking from one place to another could be short or very long, depending upon the location. This journey was not within walking distance. Maree leads them to a cable car, which drives them downward, deep into the underground caverns of the castle. They descended hundreds of feet below the castle at a very high speed. Within five minutes, they had arrived at their destination.

They exited the cable car and walked down a steep slope. After a minute or so, it leveled off, and they made a right turn. Two large electronic doors stood in front of them. Maree used her key card to open the first set of doors. The sliding doors *hiss* as they pull apart like giant elevator doors. As they enter there is a reception area, and a small office to their right, and a door to their left. They walk down a long hall, make a right, and come upon two large doors just like the ones they had entered after exiting the train. Maree presses the intercom button and speaks.

"I am here with the subjects," she says. The doors slide open instantly. As they enter, they notice a waiting area with a few chairs lining each wall.

"Wait here!" Maree commands. "The Wizard will be right out." Maree walks through the sliding doors just ahead and disappears.

"Oh my God," Henry complains, "this is so fucking stressful that we have to jump through all these hoops just to talk to this guy!"

"I know," Suzanne responds calmly, "but we have gone through a lot and made it this far. We are so close!" Suzanne mentions. Just then, the doors that Maree had exited through slide open again. A man walks toward them. He is hard to identify because of the light emanating from inside the doors.

"Welcome to Oz," he says in a jolly voice and with a smile. "We have been expecting you!"

Chapter 8 – Nonnegotiable

The Offer

Suzanne and Henry are at their wit's end and are ready for anything at this point. Although they are desperate to return home, they are in no way trying to show any weakness or vulnerability. They approach this as a negotiation. Suzanne knows two things that she can fall back on. The first is that she has been prophesized as the savior of Oz. The second is that she has been sent to the castle by the Wizard's two most important allies, the good witches. She thought to herself that she would only call upon these trump cards if absolutely necessary. After twenty minutes, the doors that Maree had exited slide open once again (hiss). They see the shape of a person walking toward them as a bright light shines behind him, causing only the figure's silhouette to be seen.

"Welcome to Oz," he says in a jolly voice and a smile. "We have been expecting you!" The sliding doors close behind him (hiss), and the man comes into view. Walking toward them is a short older White male with a wrinkled face and cheerful demeanor. He wears a red three-piece suit, minus the jacket, with a black bowtie. Instead of wearing the matching suit jacket, he is wearing a white lab coat. "I am *Barkley*," he announces, "The Wizard's top advisor."

"We are here to see the Wizard," Suzanne insinuates.

"Oh, my dear, no one can see the Wizard," Barley replies. "But I promise you, I speak for him and his best interests."

"You mean we have come all this way, and the Wizard won't even see us personally?" Henry asks out of frustration.

"Tis nothing personal," Barkley responds. "The Wizard doesn't see anyone. He has his reasons." Suzanne and Henry look at each other as if they are being disrespected by the Wizard. "So, what can the Wizard do for you today?"

"We are from California, and we were

told that the Wizard can help us get back there," Suzanne explains.

"I see, I see," Barkley replies. "You know, Oz is a lovely place to live, and you are a hero here. Why would you want to return home?"

"This is not our home," Henry retorts.

"We both have loved ones and friends who are no doubt devastated by our disappearance," Suzanne cries. "We have lives there, and we must return."

"Hm, seems we have a bit of a dilemma on our hands," Barkley says somberly.

"So, you are saying the Wizard can't help us get home?" Suzanne asks, puzzled by his indifference.

"Well, not necessarily," Barkley replies.

"Either he can or cannot help us," Henry responds irritably. "Which is it?"

"The Wizard said he will help you get home, indeed," Barkley says. Suzanne smiles. Henry flashes a look of distrust.

"What's the catch?" Henry asks.

"There is no catch, per se," Barkley mentions. "Well, I wouldn't call it a catch.

But there is one small thing the Wizard asks in return for your safe passage home."

"And what might that be?" Henry asks firmly.

"You must kill the West Which and bring back her ring as proof," Barkley says. Suzanne gasps.

"Small thing!?" Henry shouts. "You gotta be fucking kidding me!"

"This is outrageous!" Suzanne cries. "Surely there must be something other than that we can offer in exchange?"

"I'm sorry, but the Wizard said this is nonnegotiable," Barkley replies. "I tried to counsel him on other alternatives, but he remained steadfast that it is this or you can remain in Oz forever."

"Great, so he sends us on a death mission!" Henry barks. "Either we stay here or get killed by the West Witch! Great fucking choices. Have you seen that God-damned flying lion she has? How about that robot on steroids waiting to ax our asses to death? If not them, how the hell will we even get by their guards? And God knows what other surprises that evil freak has up her sleeve. This is straight bullshit!" Henry is beyond irate and starts pacing around the room. Seeing Henry beginning to spiral, Suzanne needs to make a move.

"Can you give us a minute to think it over?" she asks.

"Sure, take your time," Barkley says. "I will be back in a few minutes." Barkley leaves the room. Suzanne takes a few seconds to think it over. Henry is still pacing and now talking to himself in a low, agitated voice. The moment is quite overwhelming.

The situation was always dire, but at least before, they had hope, even if it was false hope. However, at this point, the choice to stay in Oz and never return home was becoming a no-brainer instead of attempting to assassinate an almost Godlike creature, among other daunting obstacles.

"What should we do?" Suzanne asks Henry. Her question snaps him out of his daze and back into the moment.

"What should we do?" Henry asks sarcastically. "Is that a real question?"

"Don't get mad at me, Henry! I am just as upset and emotional about this as you are."

"Ok, I'm sorry, Suzanne, but do we

really have much of a choice here?" Henry asks.

"Well—"

"Well, what?" Henry shouts. "You think you and I can kill those things? You've been watching too many fucking movies. I got news for you, I ain't *John Wick*, and you ain't *Wonder Woman!*"

"Ok, well, I guess we can just stay here then," Suzanne says calmly. "I mean, it could be fun, at least for a while."

"What you mean, for a while?" Henry asks.

"Well, we do have several allies, and we will be treated like royalty," Suzanne explains. "But do you think the West Witch and her henchmen will not spend the rest of their lives hunting us down like dogs? She will have bounties on us everywhere. We won't be safe anywhere. And we will spend the rest of our short lives looking over our shoulders until one day we find ourselves in a situation we won't get out of. And she won't kill us slowly, no. We will die the most agonizing deaths. But I'm game. I will go tell him we would love to stay in Oz." Henry's face turns pale white.

"Wait, wait, wait," Henry blurts out, "not so fast." In defeat, Henry puts his head down and his right hand on his forehead. "I'm really not liking you right now," he says. Suzanne smiles. "So, we are going to fight these fools with our bare hands, just you and I?" Henrys asks.

"I will tell him that we accept the offer, but we will need weapons and a few soldiers to accompany us. They must be desperate to get rid of this witch, so they will have to compromise a bit."

"Ok, get that old dude back in here," Henry states. Suzanne waves her arms at the camera, and the doors slide open moments later. In walks Barkley.

"Have you decided?" he asks.

"Yes," Suzanne replies. "We will do it."

"Oh, great!" He exclaims.

"On one condition!" Suzanne says firmly. "We will need your finest weapons and some soldiers to accompany us on the mission!"

"That's two requests," Barkley replies, "but the Wizard would be happy to accommodate them both. I will work out the particulars with him. You three will stay the night, and we will have a *strategy session* in the morning. After that, your mission will begin."

"I need a drink or ten," Henry says, mentally exhausted.

"Yes, return to the banquet and enjoy the rest of the evening," Barkley responds. "After all, it is in your honor."

Eye Spy & The New Guy

The party is in full swing once Suzanne and Henry return. People are dancing everywhere. By now, a grand buffet of desserts and fruits have replaced the entrees. It was a joyful atmosphere overall. Henry went right for the refreshments. Within a half-hour, he was noticeably drunk. The alcohol mixed with his already somber mood transformed him into a state of incorrigible-hopelessness.

"Don't drink too much, Henry," Suzanne warns. "We need to have our wits about us tomorrow."

"Yeah, sure," Henry says sarcastically. "This is our last night on earth, or wherever the fuck this place is, so we might as well enjoy it." Henry raises his near-empty glass. "To our last Harrah!" He shouts as he chugs the remainder of his drink. "Excuse me," Henry says to the waitress standing nearby. He pauses and looks at her nametag, "*Doria*. Can I have another drink, pronto?"

"Sure thing, sir," Doria replies. A few minutes later, Doria returns with Henry's drink. However, she does not hand it to him right away. Instead, she eavesdrops on their conversation.

"So, we are just gonna stroll into the West Witch's Liar tomorrow morning with a group of wannabees and kill the witch," Henry asks. "Is that the plan?"

"He said we will have a strategy session in the morning before we attack," Suzanne reiterates. "You can ask all your questions then, Henry."

"Where is that waitress with my drink?" Henry asks as he looks around. Just then, Doria walks over to him, hands him his drink, and walks off abruptly.

Seconds later, a man walks over to Suzanne and Henry with a drink in his hand.

"So, you are the one they

prophesized, huh?" he asks.

"That's what they keep telling me," Suzanne replies.

"Oh, you have been all the rave these last couple of days," the man mentions.

"Who are you?" Henry asks.

"I am *Richard*, from your world, *Los Angeles* to be exact."

"Oh wow," Henry responds. "How long have you been here?"

"Oh, about a month or so," Richard replies. "I was on a helicopter flying over LA. Next thing I remember, I am face down in the jungle."

"How did you get to the castle?" Suzanne asks.

"Luckily, some of the queen's men found me and brought me back here. After speaking with Barkley, the Wizard found me useful and put me on as Barkley's apprentice."

"What use are you to the Wizard?" Henry asks.

"I provide him information about the technologies of our world," Richard responds. "I was an engineer back home."

"I will be right back," Henry says. "I

need a refill."

"So, I heard you are going to the West Witch's Lair tomorrow to Kill her," Richard says.

"Yeah, and we are thrilled about it," Suzanne responds sarcastically. Richard chuckles lightly.

"Well, I'm accompanying you guys!" he says. "She is one evil bitch, excuse my language, but this may be my only chance to get home."

"Oh, evil bitch suits her about right," Suzanne says. "In fact, I couldn't think of a better way to describe her! And I'm glad you will join us, but we are gonna need an army."

"Well, I'm sure that the Wizard will provide us with some of his best men for protection," Richard prognosticates. "Well, I need to turn in for the night. I will be at the strategy session in the morning, and we will make a solid plan."

"Well, thank you!" Suzanne replies. They shake hands. "It was a pleasure meeting you!"

"Likewise!" Richard says. "From what I've heard, there is no one I would rather go

into battle with than you and your team!
See you in the morning."

****

A few hours later, the party was over.
The main hall had been cleaned thoroughly.
Everyone had gone to bed for the night. The
palace was quiet and dark. Kimmie had
been sleeping soundly since she had been
escorted from the party. Henry, Suzanne,
and Kimmie each had their own rooms on
the castle's third floor, all next to one
another.

Down at the stable, a woman wearing
a hood moves cautiously so as not to be
seen. She hides as a few drunk guards walk
by, discussing the party. Once they pass,
she heads inside the stable and quietly
commandeers a horse. She walks the horse
by its reins and makes sure the coast is clear
before mounting it. She finds an unguarded
area of the compound and rides like the
wind unseen into the night.

****

She rides and rides unabated for over a few hours in complete darkness. Under cover of night, she rides up the side of a mountain via a small dirt trail. A-ways up the hill, she comes upon an entrance guarded by two soldiers. It is a large entrance carved out of the mountainside. It is the *West Witch's Lair*.

"Who goes there?" one of the guards shouts firmly. The woman removes her hood.

"It is Doria from the *Emerald City*," the woman announces. "It is one of the witch's spies!" The guards move out of the way and let her and her horse ride through. In a few moments, she reaches an area where she can park her horse. She dismounts and ties it to the wooded docking area. There to escort her to the West Witch's chambers is the Tin Soldier. After she parks her horse, the Tin Soldier turns and walks. Doria follows it, staying far behind out of fear. It leads her into the

West Witch's chamber. The Tin Soldier walks up to the doorway, steps to the side, and freezes. Doria cautiously, awkwardly walks by him and into the room.

It is the same room that the Tin Soldier had brought Shorty and the disembodied soldiers. A pentagram still rests in the middle of the floor. Water is again boiling in the black cauldron. Maura is standing over her cauldron, staring into the bubbling liquid.

"What news do you bring me?" Maura asks without removing her eyes from the boiling substance. Doria is visibly shaken, and her anxiousness shows in her demeanor. However, she is also furious and determined.

"Are my sisters ok?" Doria asks fearfully.

"Last chance," the witch says. "What news do you bring me?" the witch reiterates.

"The Wizard has ordered the one who killed your sister and her friends to attack and kill you at dawn," Doria explains. The witch snappishly looks up at Doria.

"You are sure of this?" the witch asks.

"I am positive," Doria responds. "I overheard them talking at the feast."

"Is there anything else?" asks the witch.

"That is all I know," Doria pleads, "I swear! Can I please see my sisters now?"

"If you cross me, you will not live to regret it!" the witch warns. "But first, I will make you watch your sisters suffer and die a painful death in the most horrifying manner you can think of!"

"I swear, your majesty," Doria begs. "I would never dream of betraying you!"

"You will remain at the castle and report everything until I have that trouble-maker in my possession. Then I will release your sisters."

"I will do whatever is necessary," Doria responds submissively. "Can I please see my sisters; please, I beg you?" Maura grabs her by her hair and cuts off a chunk of it. Doria has a frightened look on her face but remains calm.

"Take her to the prisoners," the witch dismissively commands of the Tin Soldier as she glibly makes an indifferent gesture with her right hand.

****

Moments later, they arrive at the dungeon. It is damp, dark, and smells like death, vomit, urine, and feces all around. The Tin Soldier again leads her to a doorway and then steps aside. Doria walks in and finds a large hallway of jail cells. Moans and groans from several prisoners fill the air. Eerie sounds of pain, neglect, and suffering are rampant. Some rush to the bars when they hear a person walking down the hallway. Some anticipate food. Some are just reacting to the unknown sounds, anticipating a loved one or a break in the loneliness. Some have just gone crazy from neglect, malnutrition, and abuse. As Doria walks down the hallway, more and more people awake and start making strange noises. Some ooh and ahh. Others scream random obscenities. The plethora of strange noises because of her presence unnerves her.

"*Mona! Shera!*" Doria begins calling-out as she walks down the hallway. She makes a left and enters another hallway. "Mona! Shera!" she continues. The jail cells seem to be endless. Coming upon the third section of cells, she hears a woman call out, "Doria?"

"Mona?" she replies.

"Doria, over here!" the voice responds. Doria runs to the end of the hallway amidst the creepy howling and moaning. There, she sees her sister, Mona, grabbing onto the bars.

"Mona!" she screams. It is the blonde that the witch had dangling from her ropes earlier. Doria begins tearing up immediately. She looks behind Mona and sees Shera unresponsive on the floor by the wall. "Oh, my God, what happened to Shera?" Doria cries.

"She is not doing well, Mona replies. "We need to get her help soon!"

"I promise, I am doing everything I can to get you out of here!" Doria pleads. "Tell her that she needs to hang in there! This should all be over tomorrow!"

"I will do my best," Mona says, looking disheveled herself. Her lips are dry and cracked. "They are not exactly taking care of any of us down here. We barely get any water, and the witch put her brand on me earlier!"

"She what?" Doria exclaims. Mona shows her the mark where the witch branded her earlier. "That sick bitch! I swear I will—"

"Shh," Mona blurts out. "We are in enough trouble, please!" Doria sighs and composes herself.

"I need water for them immediately!" Doria screams to a nearby guard, who doesn't budge. "I said, I need water, now, or I am not reporting anything else to Maura." The guard reluctantly grabs a bucket of water and hands it to Doria. Prisoners in the surrounding cells see the water being given and start banging on their cages in protest. They are dying of thirst as well! Doria scoops out some water with the ladle and holds it to the bars. Mona opens her mouth like a starving animal and sucks down a few spoons of water. Doria hands Mona the ladle filled with water. Mona carefully walks it back to Shera. She holds her head up and forces it to her lips and gently tilts it. As the water touches her lips, Shera appears to come alive. She sucks it in instinctually as a survival technique. Mona returns to the cage a few more times to refill the ladle with water, then feeds more to Shera. The water seems to help her regain some strength momentarily.

"I will be back here tomorrow to free you, I swear!" Doria promises. With that, she is off and returns to the castle before anyone notices that she is missing.

It was all a dream

Back at the castle, Suzanne is tossing and turning, having a hard time sleeping. Her eyelids finally get heavy, and she begins getting drowsy. Moments later, Suzanne awakens, lying on her stomach in a field of low-cut grass. Her eyes open slowly. She raises her head and looks around in confusion. She stands to her feet and sees a dense forest ahead with trees abnormally high. A figure appears covered from head to toe by a black veil. Her facial features behind the veil are indistinguishable. Although, the figure does strongly resemble a female. The figure is floating slowly and gracefully, about twenty yards into the forest. Curious, Suzanne walks toward her.

"Hello?" she calls out. As Suzanne approaches her, the woman begins walking backward at the same pace Suzanne is approaching. Suddenly, the woman in the veil slides left behind a tree. Suzanne loses sight of her momentarily. Suzanne picks up the pace, heading for the tree behind which the woman had disappeared. She looks around the tree when she reaches it, but the woman is gone.

"Suzanne!" she hears. It is an eerie, deep female whisper with a chorus effect. Suzanne turns around and sees the woman in the veil behind her, in the direction in which she had just traveled from. Puzzled, Suzanne calls out to her.

"Who are you?" However, the woman disappears again.

"Suzanne!" the creepy voice calls out three more times. Suzanne starts looking around in all directions trying to spot the woman.

"Who are you?" Suzanne cries. "What do you want?" The woman is nowhere in sight. Suzanne turns around quickly. Standing less than a foot away from her is the woman in the veil.

"Your death!" the woman shouts as she pulls up the veil exposing her facial features. It's the West Witch's disfigured and decrepit face. Suzanne is startled and screams.

After one blink of her eyes, Suzanne notices that she is in a cave. There is a metal bowl by her feet filled with water that looks like a dog's bowl. Suzanne takes a step forward. She goes to take another step, but she is pulled back to the rocky dungeon wall by the chains that bind her hands and legs.

"What the fuck!" she utters as she notices her restraints. She pulls on them a few times but soon realizes she is firmly detained.

Suddenly, a black figure moves so quickly across the room (from right to left) that Suzanne barely gets a glimpse of it before it disappears into the shadows.

"Did you think you could kill my sister and get away with it?" the voice says, sounding like the woman wearing the black veil earlier.

"But I didn't mean to, I swear!"

Suzanne exclaims. Just then, the West Witch darts quickly from the shadows and, in a fraction of a second, stands in front of Suzanne, facing her.

"I didn't mean to; I didn't mean to!" the witch mocks her. "Well, I'm going to mean to when I slit you from belly to throat and gut you like a pig!" Suzanne is overcome with fear. "I know you're coming to me. I'll be waiting!" Maura starts laughing manically as Gideon the lion enters the room. He saunters toward Suzanne. His pace steadily increases until he is in a furious sprint toward her. Suzanne starts screaming frantically. Gideon gallops closer and closer. He opens his mouth, exposing his sharp teeth that can tear through bone like it was paper. Gideon leaps toward her! Suzanne braces herself by closing her eyes, wincing, and turning her head to the right.

Suzanne's eyelids pop open. She sits up abruptly and is screaming. She is drenched with sweat in her bed. It is still dark outside. Henry had already rushed through her door and arrived at her bed as this sequence was unfolding. She had been screaming for a minute or so already. He sits on the bed next to her.

"Are you alright?" Henry shouts. "What's wrong?"

"She knows we're coming!" Suzanne says matter-of-factly.

"Who?" Henry asks.

"The West Witch!" Suzanne says dauntingly. "She's waiting for us!"

Chapter 9 – Mission Impossible

Preparing for Battle

Morning arrives before anyone is ready for it. Then sunlight assaults the shade-less windows like an unwanted guest barging through the door with a bullhorn. The sunlight may as well be a megaphone wielded by a drill sergeant. Especially for Henry and Kimmie, who had both drank more than their fill the night before. Maree had the duty of waking up Suzanne and informing her that it was her responsibility to rally the other two. Suzanne now had the unfortunate task of waking up Henry and Kimmy after a hard night of partying and motivating them to go on a suicide mission. Suzanne steps into the hallway.

Thump!

She bumps shoulders with a female.

"Excuse me," Suzanne says politely as

she turns and faces the woman.

"I must speak with you!" the woman says definitively.

It is Doria!

"Can it wait?" Suzanne asks. "I really have a lot going on right now."

"You are going to want to hear what I have to say!" Doria says adamantly. "It is vital to your mission to kill the West Witch!" Suzanne's eyes open wide. She looks at Doria, squints her eyes, and agrees. "We need to talk in private. Follow me," Doria says.

****

Suzanne walks back Toward Henry's room. She has a blank stare on her face as if in deep thought over her private conversation with Doria. She knocks a few times on Henry's door but receives no answer. She slowly opens the door and looks inside. She sees Henry on his back with the covers up to his chin, still sleeping soundly. She walks into the room and over to his bed.

"Henry," she says softly. However, he

doesn't budge. "Henry, it's time to get up!" she says in a louder voice. This time, though, she gently shook his shoulder. Still, Henry doesn't move. Sensing the urgency of the moment, Suzanne welled up inside with an explosive mix of emotions. She rips off the covers, puts her mouth near his ear, and screams, "It's time to get up, Henry!" while shaking him violently. Henry opens his eyes and looks at her for a moment with disdain.

"Am I finally in hell?" he asks. Suzanne laughs.

"Not just yet, but maybe later, if you're lucky."

"I seriously dreamed that this was a dream," Henry explains. "How much sense does that fucking make?"

"The moment I make sense of any of this, you will be the first to know," Suzanne replies.

"Oh fuck!" Henry says.

"What?" Suzanne asks.

"We gotta break the news to Kimmie," he says. "I just realized; she has no fucking clue that we need to go to war today!"

"Yeah, tell me about it?!" Suzanne says. "Why do you think I woke you up first?"

"Oh, thanks a lot!" Henry sneers facetiously. Henry gets ready quickly, and they both head to Kimmie's room.

"What do you think she is gonna say?" Suzanne asks.

"Umm, fuck you! are you fucking crazy? Go fuck yourself! What the fuck happened to me last night? Something along those lines, I would think," Henry says.

"Uggh," Suzanne agrees reluctantly, "sounds about right."

Moments later, they arrive at Kimmie's room. They knock briefly, then enter seconds later. Kimmie is lying on her back, still asleep. Henry walks over to the side of the bed and gently shakes her shoulder.

"Kimmie, wake up!" he says. Kimmie's eyes open immediately. She is in a daze, staring up at the ceiling. After a few seconds, she speaks.

"Where the fuck am I?"

"Do you remember anything from

last night?" Henry asks.

"Yeah, I remember you being a pain in the ass and telling me not to drink that *Blitzky* crap," she says. "Nothing after that." Kimmie pauses for a moment. "Oh fuck, I guess you were right!" Suzanne and Henry start laughing.

"You were a mess!" Suzanne says.

"You were other worldly wasted," Henry says. Kimmie sits up on the bed.

"Did you'll meet with the Wizard guy?" Kimmie asks. Henry and Suzanne look at each other with reluctant gazes. Kimmie notices. "What is it?" she asks. There is another moment of silence. "Well, did you?" Kimmie asks angrily.

"Well, apparently, no one is allowed to see the Wizard, but we met with his top advisor," Suzanne mentions.

"And?" Kimmie asks impatiently.

"And he said that if we want to get home, we must first kill the West Witch today!" Henry explains.

"Stop fucking around," Kimmie says. "It is way too early for jokes!"

"We are not fucking around," Suzanne says.

"Have you both lost your fucking minds?" Kimmie asks. "I'm not going anywhere! Let me talk to this Wizard asshole! I will straighten him out!"

"Look, Kimmie, we can either do this or stay in Oz and be hunted for the rest of our days by the witch," Henry says. "She will never stop hunting us. And, if we manage to evade her for a while, think of all the other things here than can kill us. Shit, we almost got eaten by alligator sharks, or whatever the fuck those things were."

"Look," Kimmie says firmly, "you ball-sacks wake me up—I'm hungover as a mother fucker; I mean, I feel like a truck hit me, then backed up over me, then drove over me again—to tell me that we need to kill some demon bitch? Nah, I'm good! I will take my chances here!"

"But Kimmie, this place is not for us!" Suzanne says obstinately.

"It's more for me than getting killed by some exorcist chick!" Suzanne looks at Henry.

"What do you want me to do?" Henry says to Suzanne. "If she doesn't wanna go, she doesn't wanna go!"

"Can you at least attend the strategy session with us?" Suzanne asks. "At least you will hear what the plan is, and you can decide then."

"Oh, I've already decided," Kimmie responds. "But I will attend your stupid strategy session," Kimmie says as she gestures with each of her first two fingers, forming quotation marks. "It may be the last time I see you guys again."

"Great, thanks for being so supportive, Kimmie," Henry says facetiously.

"Anytime!" Kimmie states.

"Get ready," Suzanne says. "We meet in a half hour. And trust me; I have a plan!"

"What plan?" Henry asks.

"Just trust me!" Suzanne says.

****

The strategy session takes place on the fourth floor, overlooking the lake at the back end of the palace. A large rectangular-shaped wooden table made of rustic redwood and juniper roots rests in the middle of the room. As the crew enters,

Barkley is standing at the table with three gentlemen. Henry walks in first, followed by Suzanne. Kimmie is trailing far behind. As Henry and Suzanne walk in, Barkley introduces the other three men.

"Good morning!" Barkley says cheerfully. "This is *General Gerns*, one of the four leaders of the Queen's army. Next to him is *Dr. Monte*, our resident geographer. He knows this land and the terrain like no one else. And finally, Richard, our resident engineer, whom you've met and will be accompanying you on this trip. Where is your third member?" Just as he asks, Kimmie walks in. She has her head down, still severely hung over and indifferent to the meeting at hand. Richard looks up at her, and his face immediately changes from calm and collected to looking like he sees a ghost. His jaw drops. His mouth opens wide, along with his eyes. Kimmie slowly looks up. The look on her face immediately changes from detached to shockingly engaged. Richard and Kimmie lock eyes, and for a moment, they are speechless. Kimmie breaks the silence.

"Richard?" she calls out in a

desperate, crackly voice.

"Oh my God, is that you, Kimmy?" he shouts. The two rush toward each other. The others in the room are caught entirely off guard. However, they all feel the tension in the room, which is so thick they need to wipe it away from their eyes. The two embrace firmly. Kimmie's eyes fill with tears. Suzanne looks at Henry.

"Oh my," she says. "That's her boyfriend; the one she spoke of when she told us about their helicopter ride that led them here."

"Holy cow, that's right!" Henry says. The others hear Suzanne's explanation and look on fondly. They break the embrace and look into each other's eyes.

"I thought I lost you!" Kimmie cries.

"Me too, my love!" Richard replies softly.

"But, how are you here now?" Kimmie asks in confusion.

"We have much to catch up on," Richard replies. "But first, we have a mission to accomplish before we can get home and resume our lives."

"Please tell me that you are not going

on this suicide mission with these crazy people?" Kimmie asks.

"We can't stay here, Hun," says Richard. "We don't belong here."

"Surely, we can make a life here together now that we found each other," Kimmie suggests. "I don't wanna lose you a second time!"

"I gave them my word. I am going with them," Richard says. "I am all in on this mission. Sometimes, you gotta stand and fight for what is right, no matter the consequences." They hug again tightly.

"Excuse me?" Barkley says. "We have an important mission in a couple of hours, and we must prepare. Can we save the dramatics until we are done?"

Briefing

Everyone is gathered around the glossy wooden table with two maps laid out. The first is the complete map of Oz. The second is a map of just the west area of Oz. Dr. Monte starts with the full map. The Emerald City lies dead center, in the middle of Oz. Although the *West Witch's Lair* is pretty much a straight path to the west via the *Red Brick Road*, Dr. Monte suggests an alternate route in order to make a more covert entrance. He recommends they travel north/west, crossing onto the northern side of the *Red Brick Road*. He switches to the west map and points to the mountain that holds the *West Witch's Lair* atop it. He points to the base of the hill, which lies in the lower-left area of the mountainside, and explains that there is an entrance to an *abandoned mine*, which he theorizes leads to the lair. Moreover, he explains, the entrance to the mine is unguarded.

"There is an abandoned mine at the southern base of the mountain, far below the entry point to the witch's lair." Dr. Monte says as he directs his wooden pointer to the location on the map that is pinned to a cork bulletin board using thumb tacks. "At the mine's entrance, there is a chain-link gate that likely has a padlock that requires a key. Therefore, you will need to equip a bolt cutter. Once inside, there are several different tunnels and pathways that split off and lead to different areas of the mine. I have an old layout of the mine's interior here." Dr. Monte unpins the west map and replaces it with the historical map of the mine. "Keep in mind that this is an old map, and the current configuration might be vastly different due to collapses or deterioration as the mine has not been seen or maintained for many years."

"Great!" General Gerns says. "So, we are basically going in blind. And, any blockage will completely negate the purpose of this old map?"

"Unfortunately, that may be the case," Dr. Monte says regretfully. "However, regardless of that option, there is only one other entrance known to lead to the witch's lair, and that is the front entrance. You must find a way through any obstacles in the mine and locate the lower entrance to the lair." Kimmie rolls her eyes in frustration. "I have made two copies of the map," Dr. Monte explains. "Please choose wisely who will carry them."

"I will carry one of them, the general proclaims. "Suzanne should carry the other as she is our best chance to kill the witch. We must protect her at all costs; with our lives if we must!"

"You must be very careful of several things as you enter the mine," the doctor asserts. "Due to lack of maintenance, the cave is very unstable. There may be falling debris and blockages. Be very mindful when firing weapons as this could cause the cave to collapse on top of you." Kimmie looks at Suzanne and grimaces. "Also, be careful of large cracks and gaps in the cave floor. The person leading the way should hold a flashlight and be extremely cautious of the ground ahead."

"We are so fucked!" Kimmie mentions adamantly to Suzanne, who is still clearly shaken from the dream she had the night before.

"Any questions?" Dr. Monte asks. Kimmie raises her hand.

"Yes?" asks the doctor.

"Can talking loud cause a cave-in as well?"

"I can't answer that," the doctor replies. "I have no data regarding the condition of the mine. However, I suggest keeping conversations to a whisper and only speaking on mission strategy. The likelihood that the cave will collapse on you randomly without any provocation is extremely low."

"How low are we talking?" Kimmie asks.

"A fraction of a percentage, if I had to guess," the doctor presumes.

The briefing ended at noon. The Wizard had decided that he would provide the crew with their choice of weapons and assistance from *Battalion 12*, which consists of *twenty soldiers* from the *Queen's army* led by *General Gerns*. After a very successful strategy session, the crew heads down for a buffet brunch held in their honor. Most of the people from the night before are in attendance. No one wanted to miss this historic moment. Even though most of the residents are skeptical, to say the least—many placing bets on how long the group will stay alive (*the majority leaning toward less than a twenty-four-hour death*)—there still is a glimmer of hope and jubilation surrounding the event. It is the first time in several generations that they would make an attempt to fight back against the overwhelming oppressive tyranny brought about by the *Thanatos family*!

"I believe that the witch knows we are coming," Suzanne declares.

"That is impossible!" the general emphasizes. "Why do you say this?"

"Because I had a dream last night of her, and she told me that she is awaiting our arrival," Suzanne explains.

"A dream?" the general scoffs. "It is your mind playing tricks on you!"

"I swear, it was very real," Suzanne says adamantly. "I have a bad feeling about this."

"The North Witch has a shield spell around the castle," Richard mentions. "The West Witch cannot hear or see anything that goes on inside the castle."

"Plus, we literally just made this plan up this morning," the general emphasizes. "Even if there was a spy among us, that person would not have time to relay the message to the evil one."

"I understand," Suzanne says reluctantly. "I am just telling you how I feel and that the dream was like no other dream I ever had. It was so vivid. I can taste and smell the places still."

"You also have never been in such a life-threatening scenario," the general declares. "I have been to war many times. I have seen this a thousand times before, where one of my soldiers has a false premonition." Kimmie hugs Suzanne and comforts her.

"Yes, the subconscious mind can be very persuasive in times of extreme stress," Dr. Monte insists.

"Just stay alert at all times," Suzanne advises.

Rallying the Troops

After eating, General Gerns leads everyone to the artillery room to choose their weapons for the mission. As the door opens, they are astounded by the myriad of weapons hanging in five rows on each wall. Some of the weapons they did not even recognize! Most of them were similar to what they have seen before. However, some appeared a bit more sophisticated than those which could be found on earth. The general tried to assess each of their weaponry skills. Surprisingly, most of them had some type of weapons training. The only one who had never fired a gun before was Henry. Therefore, Henry felt more comfortable choosing the machete.

Furthermore, he explained his love for the *Friday the Thirteenth* movies as the catalyst for his choice. Richard chooses the rifle, claiming he is an expert soldier in *Call of Duty* on *Play Station 5,* as he takes a swig of the bottle of whiskey. Suzanne picks the spiked mace club, a small wooden club with twenty-one metal spikes surrounding the barrel. Kimmie selects two handguns, which she holsters; one on each hip. She explains that her father used to take her to the shooting range when she was young. He always feared that there would be some sort of upheaval in her time that would require her to take up arms in order to survive. He was not an admirer of the establishment. He believed that it would eventually break down and that 'the people' would ultimately suffer for the elite's greed and their relentless desire for power.

Before they regroup with the others,

the general has some final words. He assures them that he and his troops will be at their command and are fully committed to the mission. Earlier, the Wizard had authorized the general to select *twenty members* of the *royal* army to accompany them on their assignment. As they walk to the castle's front to meet the others, Henry pulls Suzanne aside.

"You know you are going to have to give a speech to all before we depart, right?"

"A speech," Suzanne asks in confusion. "What do you mean?"

"Look," Henry says firmly, "I played in an important basketball tournament in high school. We were ranked number twelve out of sixteen teams. We just kept winning and winning until we got to the finals. There, we faced the number one team. We were huge underdogs. No one gave us a chance to win, but I believed we could beat them! I saw the look on my teammates' faces. They were just happy to be there. They didn't think we had a chance. I needed to convince them that not only did we have a chance, but we were also better than them!

We deserved it!"

"How did you do that?" Suzanne asks.

"I told them that everyone has a weakness. Everyone has a breaking point. We had nothing to lose. All the pressure was on them. The closer we kept the game, the more pressure we put on them, and the more my guys would believe that we could win and that our opponents would start to doubt themselves. The key was to not think about the big picture but for everyone to go out and do their jobs individually. Beat the man in front of them on every play! Focus only on the task at hand! I called it *'The Cumulative Effect."*

"Why did you call it that?" Suzanne asks, listening intently.

"Because I told them that if we each worry about the man in front of us on every play, these plays would make up the difference between winning and losing. We needed to compartmentalize and be like robots. It wasn't about emotion, but about focusing in on one singular thing: winning the six inches in front of your face!"

"Wow, I like that," Suzanne mentions. "I think you should give the speech."

"No," Henry says. "You are the chosen one. You are the leader, and the one everyone is looking to."

"Did you guys win that game?" Suzanne asks.

"No," Henry replies. "But we kept it close."

"Oh!" Suzanne replies, puzzled.

"Just remember to speak from the heart!" Henry proclaims. "Just remember how deep down inside, you really want to get home, and speak from that place. They will rally around you!"

Moments later, the crew met up with the twenty soldiers at the front gate. The soldiers appeared unmotivated. Several military members seemed disengaged and hopeless regarding the upcoming task. Some were looking downward, not making eye contact while conversing, others fidgeted frequently, and some had their arms crossed as they expressed their negativity toward the upcoming event.

After Henry's recent pep talk, Suzanne became hypersensitive to these body langued cues. She knew she needed to rally the troops with her passion. However, public speaking was not only one of her weakest skills; it triggered extreme panic attacks! One time for a high school assignment, while speaking in front of her class, Suzanne got so flustered that she ran out of the classroom in the middle of her presentation and was later found sitting in a bathroom stall, bawling her eyes out in shame!

As she looked outward and witnessed the many disengaged faces, she pictured herself starting a speech vigorously but quickly losing focus and getting in her own head. Her own mind was sabotaging her address even before she uttered a word. She vacillated between giving the speech and not. Suzanne is a very logical person. She must mull over different scenarios before coming to a conclusion and finally taking action. Her confidence is rooted in her preparation. However, there was no time for that! This was a do-or-die situation. Suzanne knew that she had to decide in the next couple of minutes whether to speak or not. Any words that she musters up later would be fruitless. The troops are ripe; the time is now!

"Excuse me," she says politely. The soldiers are all speaking to one another and cannot hear her. "Excuse me!" she says a bit louder. Still, they completely ignore her. *"EVERYONE! LISTEN UP!"* Suzanne screams. Everyone is caught off guard. They stop talking immediately and turns their attention to her. It was like the needle on the record player had just slid across the vinyl record.

"I know this is the last thing you wanted to do today!" she says. The soldiers approve through unintelligible chatter amongst themselves and agreeable facial gestures. "The odds of us completing this mission successfully are like, I can't even put a percentage on it, but it's probable like five percent or worse." The soldiers start looking at each other even more distressed. They are also confused, thinking, 'where is she going with this?'

"Let's be honest, we are probably gonna die today!" The crowd begins talking amongst themselves in objection to her candor. They are beginning to question the sanity of their leader. Some even start booing.

"So, what should we do?" Suzanne shouts. "Give up? Run? Hide?" Each member looks around at the others, thinking that might not be such a bad idea.

"You can run home to your families and loved ones and hold them for a few nights. Maybe even a few months. But the West Witch wakes up every day with one ambition: to rule Oz and destroy any happiness you have now or will have in the future." The soldiers casually shake their heads up and down in agreement while quietly chattering.

"How many more chances are you going to get to end this?" Suzanne shouts with confidence. Her voice is noticeably more aggressive and self-assured. "We will never be more coordinated than this. We may never have a better opportunity to end this for good! Imagine this if you will; we kill the West Witch today, and you wake up tomorrow in a liberated land!" The soldiers murmur in agreement.

"Imagine how not only will you be remembered and revered for being the conduit to this transformation, but think of how much you will have changed the lives of your children and their children!" The collective volume of the murmurs doubles. "Is that not worth your sacrifice here today? Or shall we put this burden on future generations because we are either too scared to fight back or don't believe we can win?" The crowd noise intensifies further, "No!" She cries.

"She may kill us all, that fucking scary, ugly mongrel!" Suzanne shouts angrily. Kimmie smiles and can't believe that Suzanne just sounded like her there for a second. "But she is gonna have to kill us!" The crowd is now galvanized and cheering for her! "And even if we fail, future generations will remember your sacrifice and pick up where you left off, never cowering to oppression. Therefore, if we are to fail, it will not be because we tried, but because we didn't!" The soldiers are now collectively on her side, hanging on her every word. Suzanne looks at Henry, who provides her with a quick nod of approval.

"They say my arrival was prophesized, and that I would be the one to kill the East and West Witches! Well, is the East Witch not dead?!" she screams confidently. The soldiers are feeling euphoric. "I got this ring here after killing that psycho!" Suzanne shouts as she raises the ring up high above her head. The crowd goes wild. "What do you say we go fulfill the rest of the prophecy, get that final ring, and unite this land under its rightful rulers?" The soldiers start chanting in unison, "*Prophetia, prophetia, prophetia...*" Suzanne marches forward humbly but proudly. They all follow her, never more ready for war!

Chapter 10 – Backlash

Murder For "Higher"

The West Witch is more than prepared for the upcoming offensive than the group is aware of. Suzanne and her crew are relying upon the element of surprise to get to her. However, they are unaware that Doria had prewarned the evil one of their plans. Suzanne, Henry, Kimmie, Richard, the general, and twenty of his soldiers covertly march over the *Red Brick Road* and across the western border.

The West Witch stands above a boiling cauldron as she mutters an unintelligible phrase, then takes the chunk of Doria's hair she had retrieved earlier and tosses it into the pot. "Let her presence and what she speaks of remain unseen." Within a few seconds, black smoke rises from the cauldron and takes the form of a snake. The smoke shoots out the window as if someone had thrown a black-smoking javelin. It is out of sight within seconds. It travels to the edge of the western territory and then takes the shape of a black basketball with a hole in the middle. The hole serves as a camera, projecting the surrounding images back into the liquid in the witch's cauldron. The witch can now see anything the smokey surveillance camera picks up. Within a few minutes, the witch focuses on Suzanne and the group accompanying her as they cross into the western territory. She knows their exact location and sees their movements. The smoke-filled surveillance camera is unseen by the oncoming army as it floats above the trees. The West Witch summons a pack of zombie-wolves to attack the approaching resistance.

Suzanne and her group are walking through the dense forest on their way to the Witch's Lair. The soldiers are leading the way. Suzanne and Henry are walking together behind them. Kimmie and Richard are walking together, holding up the rear, and are distracted. They spend most of the walk catching up on what the other had been doing since their unexpected separation. The group had already been walking for a couple of hours. The time is 2:30 p.m. General Gerns is marching just behind his men and a few feet in front of Suzanne and Henry.

"General?" Suzanne calls out. The general stops and turns. "How much longer until we reach the Witch's Lair?"

"We should arrive in approximately *two hours*. Just before sunset."

"Ok, thank you," Suzanne responds. She looks at Henry. "How you holding up?"

"I'm surprisingly calm for the last day of my life," Henry says flippantly.

"That's not funny!" Suzanne responds. "We have back up. We have a good plan. We are gonna do this."

"I know," Henry responds. "I am just suppressing my emotions and staying focused. I'm kind of numb right now and just trusting in the process."

"Just think, before you know it, you will be playing in the NBA, and you better send me tickets when I ask for them!" Henry giggles.

Kimmie looks at Richard with a serious look on her face. "I'm just happy I found you, boo!" Richard says.

"I would have never gone on this mission if you were not going," Kimmie asserts. "I still think this is a terrible idea."

"Kimmie, we need to fight to get home!" Richard avows. "We don't belong here! Furthermore, you and I had plans back home. We both want to get married and have a family. What kind of family will we raise here? And will we ever get to that point with this evil targeting us? In this land, we have predators. We are not at the top of the food chain here!"

"Well, there is no use arguing about it now," Kimmie says. "We are already pot committed."

"Oh, I see I did teach you something about Texas Hold'em," Richard says in jest.

"You always say I don't listen to you," Kimmie says, "but I do!"

Suzanne approaches General Gerns.

"Are you and your men from Oz?" Suzanne inquires.

"Why do you ask?" the general replies.

"Because you all talk and act like you are like us," she explains.

"We are from *Texas*," General Gerns

explains. "We have been here for what we believe to be two years or so."

"Oh my God!" Suzanne exclaims. I knew it! You should come home with us when all this is over."

"Our duty is here now!" the general proclaims. "We are invested in this place at this point. Long gone is the attachment to our previous lives. We believe that our destiny lies here, and we have made up our minds that we will defend this place with our lives! We pledged our allegiance to the queen and believe this is our true purpose!"

Suddenly, the group hears a chorus of howling sounds in the distance. It stops them in their tracks.

"What the fuck was that?" Kimmie shouts.

"Sounds like a few wolves," Suzanne mentions calmly. "No need to worry. We have numbers, and we are armed."

"True, but we have seen some crazy shit here so far," Henry proclaims. "I've seen an alligator with a shark's fin. How do we know those are wolves?"

"Let's just stay together and keep moving forward," the general suggests.

First Offensive

After another few miles of marching, General Gerns orders a stop-march and commands that they set up camp for some much-needed food, water, and rest before pushing forward. Everyone agrees that a brief rest would do them all good. The black ball surveillance camera watches as the group sets up campfires and a rest area. Eight guards patrol the borders of the encampment, two in each direction (*two north, two south, two east, and two west*). They set up several small tents within the small perimeter.

Small grills cooked food that fed many of the hungry soldiers. They planned to rest for about an hour after eating before resuming their invasion. After an hour or so, the camp is relatively calm and quiet. Many soldiers are taking a cat nap to conserve their energy for what might be an all-night offensive. Being a covert infiltration mission, the goal was not time-sensitive. Instead, the strategy was more like a hunting expedition, sitting quietly in the bush and waiting as long as needed to catch a deer off guard.

However, they did not know that zombie-wolves were currently surrounding them on all sides and getting ready to attack. The witch had summoned the undead wolves from the earth via an ancient spell. It was easy to tell that they were not alive with just a glance. Most had their ribs exposed due to the absence of skin around their mid-sections. Others had exposed skeletal faces for the same reason. Some are salivating from their mouths, and they are ultra-aggressive, not only because of the spell the West Witch had put on them, but because they crave living human blood!

Two guards on the north side of the camp are sitting somewhat complacent on some fallen trees. They are not expecting any combat this far from *ground zero*.

"I think we are going to catch the witch off guard and overwhelm her!" *guard-three* says.

"I agree," *guard-four* responds. "We have a great plan. I can't believe we are finally going to end this after all these years." Just then, guard-three sees movement up ahead between the trees. She wasn't sure as it was more of a blur than anything she could recognize or confirm.

"Did you see that?" she asks nervously.

"See what?" guard-four asks.

"I swear I saw something moving over there," guard-three points ahead.

"I didn't hear or see anything," guard-four responds. "I think your mind might be playing tricks on you."

"Maybe you're right," guard-three agrees.

"I gotta take a piss," guard-four says.

"I should go with you," suggests guard-three. "We should stick together."

"If you wanna take a look at my private part, you should just ask," guard-four says sarcastically. "I would respect you more."

"I'm serious," guard-three affirms. "We should stick together like the general said."

"I will be gone for two minutes," guard-four replies. "Stop being such a drama queen."

"Ok, but hurry up!" guard-three commands.

"I will be back in two shakes of a lamb's tail," guard-four responds.

Guard-three sits in silence as guard-four walks out of sight.

Guard-four walks a few feet into the woods and out of view. He leans his weapon against the tree trunk in front of him, pulls his pants down, and begins urinating. He lets out a sigh of relief as the built-up urine streams from his body. The sound of a strong stream of piss striking dry leaves resonates.

Suddenly, guard-four hears a low growl. The sound startles him enough that he pees on his pants a bit as he clenches up immediately and focuses on his hearing.

"Hello?" he asks. "Who is there?" He pauses for a moment to listen but hears nothing. He resumes urinating. Just as he relaxes again, he hears rapidly approaching footsteps. A wolf moves so quickly in his direction that he doesn't have time to react. It leaps forward, opens its mouth, and grabs hold of his dangling penis. Before guard-four can even process the situation, the wolf clamps down and pulls back, ripping his penis from his body. Guard-four is in such shock that he can't even scream. He looks down as if what had just happened was a dream. It was surreal. He sees blood squirting out of where his penis was only moments earlier.

Before he can react, another wolf charges from behind, grabs hold of his left leg, and begins gnawing on it. As he looks down, another wolf charges, springs up off its hind legs, and grabs him by the throat with its teeth. Guard-four falls to the ground, and the three feral creatures pounce on him and quickly dismember him amidst a chorus of grunts, growls, chomping teeth, and tearing flesh.

Guard-three is waiting impatiently for her partner to get back. As time passes and guard-four does not return, she is on edge and beginning to worry. She decides to go look for him. However, she does so in a stealthy fashion. She arms herself, holding her rifle in the ready position as she heads in her counterpart's direction. Seconds later, she finds her partner's rifle on the ground. She immediately starts breathing heavily as she looks around anxiously. She has an awful feeling about what she will find. She takes a few more cautious steps ahead, only to find a canteen, which she knows belongs to her partner. If that wasn't nerve-racking enough, she finds blood on some of the leaves nearby. Panic sets in. She knows that something is not right.

She turns to head back toward the camp to get reinforcements. However, just as she does, she sees three zombie-wolves growling at her lowly and showing their teeth aggressively. The one to the far-left charges first. Guard-three fires and hits it with three shots in its mid-section, sending it sliding off to the left momentarily. The other two had started charging her only a second after the first. Before she could even react with an appropriate response, the zombie-wolf on her far-right lunges toward her.

Bang!

She shoots it in the head, which stops it permanently. The one in the middle jumps toward her almost as soon as she fired the shot. It grabs hold of her left arm with its teeth and sinks them in deep. She drops her gun inadvertently. The wolf on the left, whom she had shot, springs back up and joins the feeding, springs back up and joins the feeding. Both wolves start gnawing on her flesh aggressively. She lets out several horrifying screams but soon loses consciousness. Seven more wolves emerge and charge the breeched location leading into the camp. After striping guard-four's bones clean, the other two follow the pack.

Hearing the shots fired from guard-three, all remaining crew members awaken, spring up, grab their weapons, and assemble at the front of the camp where the screams were heard. They assemble just in time to find the remaining nine zombie-wolves charging at them relentlessly. Most of them are still groggy from waking up so suddenly moments earlier. The wolves take advantage and attack without delay. Before the soldiers realize what they are facing, one of the wolves absorbs a shot and, without flinching, tackles the shooter and begins ripping and chewing flesh from his neck.

The wolves are so fast that direct shots to the head are few and far between. Moreover, the group hasn't had time to realize that they are fighting zombie-wolves and that the only thing that will stop them is a headshot. Another soldier is taken down from behind by a wolf chomping on his leg. Another pounces from the front, and they both quickly dismember the soldier's face. The surprise they were supposed to bring to the West Witch had been brought to them instead.

Henry rounds up Suzanne and Kimmie (who happens to be with Richard). As they exit their tent, they wittiness the carnage taking place all around them.

"This way!" Henry shouts. The three of them run toward the woods in the opposite direction of the attack. Six more of the queen's guards rush past them, moving in the opposite direction in an effort to ward off the attackers. During their escape, a wolf lunges toward Suzanne.

Bang!

Henry shoots it in the head and watches it fall lifeless to the ground. Kimmie uses the butt of her rifle to strike another attacking wolf in its jaw. As it hits the ground and tries to recover, Kimmie turns the gun on it and fires.

Boom!

She blows its head clean off at close range. The sounds of tormented soldiers screaming fill the air. Within a few moments, it was all over. They could tell by the deafening silence. They assembled back at the campsite. Ten dead wolves and six dead soldiers covered the area.

General Gerns wasted no time in ordering grave digging to bury the fallen. Once completed, he ordered them to march forward. Morale is low after the attack, but many are angry. Six soldiers were killed violently. However, there was little time to think about the dead as they aggressively marched toward the Witch's Lair.

Don't "Mine" Me

After crossing back over the *Red Brick Road*, the group heads for the south corner of the mountainside. After only a few minutes, they reach the entrance to the abandoned mine. The general orders one of his soldiers to cut the padlock with the bolt cutters.

Snap!

The lock is removed easily, and they open the fence gates. The group has successfully infiltrated the lowest level of the lair. Even though they lost six soldiers, morale is building again as their plan is slowly coming together. Still, they have a bit of trepidation regarding the reliability of the map leading them in the right direction. There are mine railway tracks leading to the left and to the right. The general browses the blueprints briefly. Everyone is equipped with a flashlight, which was a great idea seeing that it is pitch black inside the cave.

"I heard that the *Trap Door Spiders* live in this area," *Commander (CDR) Jawa* announces to the group.

"The what?" General Gerns asks.

"The deadliest spider in the world," CDR Jawa asserts.

"How do you know that?" the soldier wearing the *blue bandana, Corporal (CPL) Ney,* asks sarcastically.

"Jawa went to school as an arachnologist," the general explains. "I would take him seriously.

"A what?" *CPL Ney* asks in confusion.

"That's a person who studies spiders and other arachnids," Henry explains.

"Ok, so we should be scared of spiders now?" the soldier wearing the *black scarf* (*soldier-three*) says arguably.

"Yeah, you should be," CDR Jawa says firmly.

"Why the hell should we be afraid of a damn spider?" *CPL Ney* asks.

"Because, if you get bit by one, you will die an excruciating death in about fifteen minutes," CDR Jawa states.

"How will we know they are different from any other spiders?" Kimmie asks.

"First off, they look like tarantulas," CDR Jawa says, "but they are far worse. They are blind because they live in dark caves. You would think that this gives you an advantage. However, although they don't have ears, they have a complex set of hairs all over their bodies that are ultrasensitive to sound from the vibrations of the sound waves."

"So, we should play Marco-Polo with these motha fuckas?" Kimmie asks.

"Not at all!" CMD Jawa states. "Their senses are highly sophisticated in locating sound. So, once they are onto you, they will still be able to track you down even if you remain still."

"Then, how do we survive such an attack?" Suzanne asks.

"They usually travel in groups," he explains. "If you see a bunch of spiders, run and don't look back!"

"We need to go left," the general interrupts. No one objects. They make a left through the narrow rocky tunnel that slopes downward. Kimmie starts sweating, experiences shortness of breath, and her heartbeat speeds up.

"It's really hot in here!" Kimmie says. The further down they travel, the hotter it becomes, reaching almost eighty degrees with no air circulation. "I'm not good with condensed spaces, let alone ones that are scorching hot!" Kimmie confides in Suzanne.

"Just try and stay calm," Suzanne says.

"I can't," Kimmie responds in a panic. "I am about to lose my shit!" Suzanne remains calm.

"I understand how you are feeling," Suzanne responds, validating Kimmie's concerns. "But just think, we are gonna be home soon. We will be sitting at your favorite bar doing shots and trying to figure out what we are going to do with the rest of our boring lives, always remembering this as the most exciting time of our lives. You know why it is gonna be so exciting?"

"No, please enlighten me?" Kimmie asks sardonically.

"Because nothing we do for the rest of our lives will ever compare to this!" Suzanne explains. "This is our shining moment; our destiny. Anything after this will be anticlimactic cause this is what we were born for!"

"Ok, good speech," Kimmie says. "You almost have me convinced. But you definitely have me motivated. Let's kick some ass! I'm ignoring the limited space around me," Kimmie says as she winces and tries hard to think of something positive. They soon arrive at a fork in the road. They have traveled almost one thousand feet below the entrance of the mine.

"We need to go left," the general says. Just then, a scarecrow looking precisely like the one in the cornfield appears twenty yards in front of them.

One of the soldiers sees it and begins firing. This sets off the other soldiers, who begin firing as well at the ominous figure. Suddenly, the cave starts shaking.

"Ceasefire!" the general screams. A few more rounds pop off before the firing stops completely. The mine makes an eerie rumbling noise just before it collapses!

Crash!

The cave collapses on top of the group! Several terrifying screams sound off as large rocks and debris fall from the ceiling, causing a smokey mist in its aftermath. A chorus of thuds can be heard as the stones hit the ground, bounce off bodies, and crush some. Within a few seconds, there is silence.

****

As the smokey mist begins to subside, some people are heard screaming. Henry opens his eyes after momentarily being unconscious. He slowly regains his senses, brushes rocks and rubble off of himself, and stands up. He looks around.

"Suzanne!" he cries. "Suzanne!" He begins looking around frantically. He sees several body parts sticking out from underneath the debris. He urgently begins removing the rubble, searching for survivors, particularly Suzanne. As he is doing so, Suzanne pops up a few yards away, covered in debris and clearly shaken.

"Henry," she calls out.

"Oh, thank God!" Henry says aloud. "Are you ok?"

"I think so," Suzanne mentions. "Where's Kimmie?"

"I don't know," Henry says. They both move quickly, trying to dig out any survivors. Henry digs and digs around one of the soldiers whose head is buried pretty deep. When he finally pulls him free, Henry realizes the collapse has killed him. Seconds later, Suzanne yells.

"I found her!" Henry rushes over. Meanwhile, three soldiers manage to emerge from the wreckage and begin searching for survivors. Suzanne and Henry anxiously remove the rubble from Kimmie's body. She remains motionless even after they remove the debris from around her head. "Oh no!" Suzanne cries out in dread. Seconds later, Kimmie opens one eye. "Kimmie, are you ok?" Suzanne asks impatiently.

"Who the fuck thought this was a good idea?" Kimmie asks sarcastically.

"She's fine," Henry says with a sigh of relief.

"We found another casualty," *Commander Sagez* informs them, "but we have not located the others." That makes two soldiers dead thus far. However, they have not yet found the remaining soldiers, General Gerns, nor Richard.

"Ok," Henry says as he looks around, "the collapse happened here. They may be on the other side," henry states, referring to the wall of rubble between them and the way they had entered the mine, which is now blocking them from going back the way they came.

"Hello!" Suzanne screams at the wall of debris. "Is anyone there?" "Hello! Can anyone hear me?"

"Suzanne?" someone answers back.

"General Gerns?" Henry asks.

"Yes," the general replies. "Is anyone else with you over there?" the general asks.

"Yes, we have four soldiers, myself, Henry, and Kimmie," Suzanne shouts.

"We have seven soldiers and one casualty," the general announces.

"Oh, no!" Kimmie shouts as she begins to tear up. "Where is Richard?" she screams. "Richard, Richard!"

"I'm right here, my love!" Richard shouts from the other side of the wall.

"Sorry," the general laments, "Richard is also with us."

"Oh, thank God!" Kimmie says in relief.

"We have two dead soldiers on this side," Suzanne relays.

"So, that's three casualties from the mess!" the general shouts.

"What are we gonna do?" Suzanne asks.

"Do you see a way forward?" the general asks.

"Yes," Henry shouts. "There is a tunnel to our right."

"Well, follow that tunnel," the general responds. "We have a tunnel to our left. We will figure out a way to meet you, but I believe you are on the more direct path to the witch's lair."

"But we need you guys!" Kimmie's voice skreiches.

"There isn't much we can do right now but meet up later," the general acknowledges. "You must finish the mission at all costs! We have not come this far and sacrificed this many to turn back now!"

"Ok, we will!" Suzanne responds.

"Richard!" Kimmie screams.

"I'm here, my love," he responds.

"Please be careful!"

"You too, hun," he shouts. "I love you so much!"

"I love you too!" Kimmie yells. "I lost you once. I'm not losing you again!" she cries.

"See you on the other side, general!" Suzanne says.

* * * * * * * * * * * * * * * * * * * *

The general led his group through the

only tunnel that was available to them, hoping that it would somehow lead to the Witch's Lair, which was far above their location. Making matters worse, the tunnel that they traveled through leads even further down from where they are located. After exiting the narrow tunnel, they entered a more spacious area that connects to a docking station. They had a nice view of a large glass window and metal wall. Behind the window and wall appeared to be a *control room*. However, the entrance also seemed to lead to a larger facility.

"What do you say we try our luck through that door?" Richard asks the general.

"Sounds like a plan considering the track ahead looks like it's headed even further down, and we need to go up asap," the general responds. "Maybe we can even find some supplies in there."

They enter through the doorway. They bypass the control room on their right and head straight down the hallway. There, they find two doors leading in different directions.

"We need to find a stairwell that

leads up," the general announces. "Let's split up and see what we can find. *Commander (CDR) Jawa*, you are in command of *Delta Team*. Take these *three soldiers* and go that way." He points to the door on the right. I will take these three soldiers and Richard and go this way (he points to the door on the left). "We are *Alpha Team*. Meet back here in ten minutes." The soldiers set the timers on their electronic watches.

"Roger that!" Commander Jawa responds. Both teams separate immediately.

Walking Into Spiderwebs

The members of *Delta Team* shine their lights down the long, dark hallway looking for open rooms where they can quickly acquire any mission-valuable items. However, their main priority is to find a stairwell that leads up within eight minutes. That will leave them two minutes to return to the rendezvous site. Delta Team carefully walks down the hallway in combat position. Along the way, they notice a door to their right. They check to see if it is open, and it is. CDR Jawa orders *soldier-one* and *soldier-two* to enter the room and quickly acquire any mission-valuable items while he and *CPL Ney* continue down the hallway looking for stairs leading up.

CDR Jawa and *CPL Ney* continue on. They soon come upon a myriad of spider webs that cover the entirety of the remaining hallway. They can see a doorway at the end of the hall through the thick collections of webs.

"I told you those spiders are in here!"

CDR Jawa says.

"They could be harmless," CPL Ney replies. "I would be shocked if there weren't spiders in an abandoned mine."

"Just keeps your wits about you!" CDR Jawa emphasizes. They continue their methodical pace forward, with their knees bent and their weight on the balls of their feet. They wipe aside spider webs with their guns in the ready position, keeping them as steady as possible. They both hear low hissing and purring noises as they approach the door facing them.

"What the fuck was that? CPL Ney asks.

"Those are spiders!" CDR Jawa says in a panic.

"I'm going in!" CPL Ney says.

"No!" CDR Jawa shouts. However, it is too late. CPL Ney had already rushed through the door, leaving it open for him to follow.

"Oh, shit!" CPL Ney screams. CDR Jawa enters through the doorway and turns to his right. He sees CPL Ney stuck to a large, complex spider web the likes of which they had never seen before. CDR Jawa looks up and sees stairs leading up. However, he also sees thousands of *trap door spiders* charging toward CPL Ney coming from the stairs above. CDR Jawa grabs his arm and pulls him with all his might, but he won't budge. CDR Jawa gathers himself quickly and tries again. He pulls and pulls to try and break his teammate free. The deadly, ultra-aggressive spiders are closing in fast. They are on the walls above and the sides, on the web leading to CPL Ney, on the banister and railings; they are everywhere! The chorus of hisses and purrs is almost deafening. Only the clicking sounds of thousands of fast-moving spider legs pushing off of the concrete ceilings and walls rival the hisses and purrs.

With one last jerk, CDR Jawa is able to break CPL Ney free. The force of the yank sends them both to the ground. They both pop up quickly and frantically head through the door from which they had entered. Just as they get through the door, CPL Ney stops.

"What are you doing?" CDR Jawa shouts.

"I forgot my gun!" CPL Ney replies.

"Screw it!" CDR Jawa yells. However, CPL Ney had already rushed back in to retrieve his firearm. He reaches down and grabs onto the rifle's stock just as a few spiders jump onto the barrel. He shakes them off while backpedaling through the door. He feels a sharp pinch on his ankle.

"Ouch!" he shouts. He brings his right ankle up and swipes at the pain area with his right hand. He pushes off one of the spiders. It is then that he realizes he has just been bit. Thousands of spiders storm through the doors heading straight for Delta Squad. CDR Jawa had taken the liberty of continuing ahead to warn the others while CPL Ney was returning to retrieve his weapon. CPL Ney sees CDR Jawa standing at the door down the hallway holding it open with his head peering inside. It is like it is happening in slow motion for CPL Ney.

As CPL Ney sprints toward him, he sees CDR Jawa backing away from the door, frantically beckoning the other soldiers to follow him. CDR Jawa turns briefly and looks to see if CPL Ney is behind him. After confirming that he is, he turns and runs toward the rendezvous point. The other two soldiers come out of the room and look down the hallway. CPL Ney is running full speed toward them. He motions for them to run the other way! The other two soldiers bolt back toward the meeting area.

****

Alpha Team is waiting patiently as *Delta Team* comes barreling through the doors, huffing, puffing, and visibly disheveled. In his haste, CPL Ney, trailing the other three, hits the door so hard on his way out that it gets stuck and remains ajar. *Alpha Team* readies their weapons, aiming them at the door as *Delta Team* approaches.

"There is a stairwell leading up," CDR Jawa says to General Gerns. "But, remember those deadly spiders I told you about?" CDR Jawa says, trying to catch his breath. "Well, there are thousands of them heading in our direction!"

"Luckily, we found another set of stairs that leads up with no spiders," the general explains. CDR Jawa turns and looks back. He sees CPL Ney slumped over with his hands on his knees and the door open.

"The door!" he screams. CPL Ney looks up at him.

"Huh?" he says.

"The door!" CDR Jawa screams again, this time making an animated gesture toward the open door.

"Oh, shit!" CPL Ney shouts. He turns around and rushes toward the door. However, thousands of spiders come pouring out before he can get to it.

"Fuck!" CPL Ney shouts. "Run!" They all turn and run, following General Gerns to the stairwell they had found. The spiders scatter about. Several find other holes and crevasses to travel through. The group enters the other room and closes the door, barely evading the deadly spiders.

Chapter 11 – End of the Road

Sinkhole or Swim

The mine shaft that had led Suzanne and her group far underground had now started to ascend, which was a good sign. The entire group had been traveling downward prior to the collapse. At their lowest point, they were nearly a thousand feet below the mine entrance. However, temperatures still remained high.

"I'm sweating my balls off," Kimmie shouts. "Do we have any friggen clue where we are or how far till we reach the death chamber?"

"The general said that this is the fastest way to the Witch's Lair," Suzanne mentions as she refers to the map. "So, we need to just remain patient and positive and stay the course."

"I swear, you should run for politics if we ever get home," Kimmie says. "You have a way of calming people and making them believe in you with your bullshit like no other!"

"Maybe you should take a lesson from her and try to be more positive," Henry says. "What problems does your complaining solve?"

"You know what?" Kimmie says. "You may be right cause if you can be positive in an abandoned mine in Oz, wherever the fuck this is, on your way to kill the closest thing I've seen to a demon in order to get home, then either you're delusional as fuck or the luckiest person I've ever met. And from what I've seen thus far if we get home, this chick needs to buy me some lottery tickets!"

"Well, you saying 'if we get home' is about the most positive thing you've said this entire trip, so I'll take it as a compliment," Suzanne says. "And for the record, you're pretty lucky yourself, having survived all this time. Don't count yourself out and your resiliency!"

"See!" Kimmie says. "The politician got me again! You are good though cause you managed to talk me into this crazy shit! I'm tweaking right now, for real!" Kimmie starts replaying all the craziness that has happened thus far, which overwhelms her emotions. She starts tearing up and looks bewildered.

"Listen!" Suzanne shouts. "Do you wanna ever see Richard again?" Kimmie immediately snaps out of it.

"Of course I do!" Kimmie says sincerely.

"Well, man-the-fuck-up!" Suzanne shouts. "No one asked for this shit, especially not me! And I bet Richard is doing everything he can to get back to you, and you owe him the same! Think about how you would feel if he gave up. Think about the pain it would cause him, and he would somehow blame himself. He would never recover. Stay focused!" Kimmie remains silent for a moment, moved by Suzanne's words. She turns to Henry and whispers.

"I fucking love this chick! If I was gay, I would marry her!" Henry chuckles. It seemed to be just what they needed to grow closer as a group, not only to loosen up the growing tension but also to motivate them and keep their minds on the mission.

They all walk around a curve in the tracks. The four soldiers lead the way, shining their flashlights to illuminate the pitch-black tunnel. Suddenly, CDR Sagez grabs *soldier-six*.

"Woh!" he shouts. Soldier-six stops instantly from the physical contact exhibited by CDR Sagez. She looks down and sees that if she had taken one more step forward, she would have fallen down a massive *sinkhole* to her death. Her anxiety levels spike instantly as she realizes that imminent death was only a step away. CDR Sagez turns to the group.

"We have a problem," soldier-six relays. They stand aside as Suzanne, Henry, and Kimmy approach the sinkhole. A portion of the road ahead had collapsed at some point. In order to continue, each person would need to jump across to the other side. However, the problem appears to be that the ledge leading to the other side is way too far to reach by merely jumping.

"Well, what the hell do we do now, miss optimistic?" Kimmie says sarcastically. Kimmie looks down the hole. Soldier-six shines her light into the abyss. Everyone takes a peek. Most wince and turn away quickly. Kimmie whimpers.

"I believe the world record for the running-long-jump is like twenty-nine feet," Henry proclaims. "This has got to be like twelve to fifteen feet."

"I guess we need to go back and call this whole thing off!" Kimmie states.

"Go back where?" Suzanne asks. "There is no way out back there because of the cave collapse, remember?" Kimmie turns pale and starts shaking as she realizes they are at a critical impasse. Moreover, Kimmie is claustrophobic. The thoughts immediately trigger her anxiety.

"Oh my God; I'm gonna fucking pass out!" Kimmie shouts as she puts her hand on her forehead and gets dizzy.

"Wait a second," Suzanne says positively. While she shines her light across to the other side, she notices something obstructing the light. She shines it upward. "It's a rope!" Suzanne shouts.

"Where? Let me see!" Henry says. "Holy shit! It is!"

"We don't know how secure it is, though," CDR Sagez says. "That rope could have been here for twenty years. We don't know what it is attached to above or if the rock it is attached to has deteriorated to the point that it won't hold a single one of us."

So, what do you suggest?" Suzanne asks him. CDR Sagez pauses for a few moments. He seems to be at a loss. It's not every day that swinging across a sinkhole in an abandoned mine comes up in military training. Just then, soldier-six steps forward.

"I will go first and make sure it is secure!" Everyone is stunned by her bravery, especially since she is the newest and lowest-ranked soldier.

"Are you sure, private?"

"I have waited my whole life for this," she declares. "I have never been more sure!"

"Ok, Godspeed!" CDR Sagez says. "Make sure you get a good running start, and don't hesitate!" The rope is hanging in the middle between both platforms.

"I read somewhere that the average person can jump around ten feet with a running start," Henry says. "I'm not sure I believe that under circumstances of high stress. It's easy to jump with no pressure, but when a sinkhole leads to instant death, it gets much more difficult. The rope can't be more than six feet away. It should be an easy jump to the rope, on paper."

"Yes," CDR Sagez replies. "Just concentrate on grabbing the rope, nothing else. Once you have a firm grasp on it, start swinging back and forth, and don't let go until you are comfortable that you will reach the other side."

Everyone steps back against the walls, clearing a runway for soldier-six. She hands her firearm to *soldier-seven*, turns and walks back, then turns and faces the jump spot. She spits on her hands and rubs them together. She has a stone-cold look on her face as she gets in the ready position, bending her knees slightly. Her mouth shifts to a snarl as she visualizes a successful jump. She rocks back and forth three times, then takes off!

She sprints toward the edge but slows slightly just before taking her final step so as not to overjump the hole or rope. She lifts off, sailing over the sinkhole and grabbing hold of the rope. Her momentum pushes her forward. She goes with it, riding it forward, backward, then forward again. She picks up speed with every swing. On the third swing forward, she releases at the furthest point closest to the landing spot.

Thud!

She hits the ground on the other side and rolls forward. Dust kicks up, making it hard for the others to see if she is ok or not.

"Oh!" Henry shouts and winces. They wait with bated breath to see her dismount. As the dust clears, soldier-six emerges, standing on the other side, unharmed.

"Piece of cake!" she comments. They let out a collective sigh of relief and a cheer. Her confident response provides them with hope and inspiration.

"I'll go next," soldier-seven declares. He attempts the jump and makes it across in only two swings of the rope. They again cheer for his successful landing. They feel even more confident now as the second participant made it look even easier than the first. *Soldier-eight* goes next with similar success as soldier-seven. After carefully observing the first three, Henry is confident that he has it down.

"I will go last," CDR Sagez says, "just in case someone has a problem and needs help coming back this way."

"I'm ready!" Henry says. He sprints toward to edge. He hears his high school basketball coach screaming at him as he sees the vitriol in his coach's face!

"Are you gonna quit, you fucking pussy!" his coach screamed. He sees one of his *White* high school teammates mocking him as he runs the forty-yard dash.

"Run like you're running from the cops!" he shouts the racist statement as he turns to another White teammate, and they laugh aloud. Henry's face turns to a scowl. He leaps, grabs the rope, swings forward once, and releases his grip. He lands firmly on the other side like an action hero in a movie, one knee up and one knee down. The group cheers in amazement! He receives the loudest cheers and provides even more confidence for the remaining members.

"Come on, Suzanne!" he screams, sounding extremely fired-up. "You can do this! I will be right here to catch you!" Suzanne nods confidently and scowls as well. She backs up, and without much thought, she takes off! Suzanne leaps forward. She grabs the rope. However, as she swings forward, she slips down the rope. The group lets out a collective sigh. Suzanne lets out a horrific scream thinking she is going to fall. This freaks her out. Her feet get caught on the knot on the bottom of the rope, thankfully. She holds on for dear life and closes her eyes.

"Come on!" Henry screams, "you can do it, Suzanne!" He reaches out to her from the edge. "Swing!" Suzanne opens her eyes, surprised to still be alive. "Swing back!" Henry shouts. "Use your hips!" Suzanne grunts and winces as she tries to swing backward. She uses her legs and arms and gets into a rhythm.

"You can do it!" Kimmie screams. Suzanne rocks back and forth, slowly picking up speed. She grunts with fury and keeps pushing. Soon, she is vacillating wildly back and forth.

"I am going to tell you when to let go, ok?" Henry says. He watches as she swings back one last time. As Suzanne swings forward, Henry screams, "Let go, now!" Suzanne releases her grip on the rope. She glides forward. Henry reaches out and grabs her. They both fall backward onto the ground safely. Suzanne is on top of Henry, straddling him. Suzanne raises her head and looks into Henry's eyes. Henry stares back. Their eyes lock, staring at one another in a trance-like state. The bond between them had strengthened significantly over the last few hours. Henry realized at that moment that Suzanne had almost died and how much he would be lost without her. Suzanne realizes how much Henry really cares about her and would do anything to protect her. Moreover, she understood she would have never gotten this far without him.

They quickly shake it off and get back into the moment. There were still two more people that needed to get across, and Kimmie was one of them. Kimmie is pacing back and forth anxiously. She grew more and more confident as each person made it across almost effortlessly. However, Suzanne's almost failed attempt had shaken her confidence.

"I can't do this!" Kimmie says to CRD Sagez.

"You can do it!" he responds. "It's easy."

"Easy?" she asks. This seemed to be the wrong thing to say to her at the wrong time. "Did that look easy to you?" she asks regarding Suzanne's near-fatal encounter.

"Kimmie!" Suzanne shouts. "You can do this! I messed up cause I didn't believe in myself for a moment. Just stay positive. Come on!"

"I can't; I can't!" Kimmie says, now in a full panic. "This is too much for me! I'm not doing it!" Kimmie states. "Not a chance!"

"How bout if you jump on my back and I carry you across?" CDR Sagez asks.

"You would do that and risk your own life for me?" Kimmie asks.

"We will make it," he responds. "I promise."

"Ok, if you say so," Kimmie replies reluctantly. He bends down. She hops on his back. She puts her arms around his shoulders and locks her hands together in a tight grip. She rests her legs around his waist. He puts his arms around her legs, securing them to his body.

"I'm gonna count to three and go," he explains, just to make Kimmie feel more comfortable.

"I'm closing my eyes," Kimmie responds. "Do what you gotta do!"

"Just hang on tight!" he says. "One, two..." suddenly, they hear loud hissing and purring sounds, which throws off their plan. CDR Sagez turns and sees a plethora of spiders aggressively rushing down the hallway toward them. Kimmie looks back.

"Oh shit!" she screams. More spiders crawl in from the cracks in the cave above. CDR Sagez takes off running. Several spiders drop down from above and in front of them. He slows slightly and sidesteps several spiders. He tries to pick up speed again but is not running very fast due to the evasive maneuver he performed to avoid them.

He leaps from the ledge!

It's like it is happening in slow motion to the others, who watch as the two appear to remain airborne for longer than they actually are. The others wince as CDR Sagez reaches out and barely grabs the rope. None of them thought that they would make it this far after the spiders appeared. As CDR Sagez hangs on the rope, several spiders begin crawling down it from above. He frantically swings back and forth to gain momentum for the jump forward. The spiders are approaching fast. The extra weight from Kimmie causes him to rock back and forth a few extra times. Once, twice, three times, four times; still, he needs more. The spiders are closing in, climbing down the rope! Several spiders drop from above, looking to latch onto them as they swing forward for the fifth time. CDR Sagez releases. He would have liked to swing once more, but the threat was imminent. He springs forward and reaches out. The falling spiders just miss them as they sail forward. Those on the other side reach out to grab him.

Thud!

His chest hits the front side of the ledge. He keeps his arms outreached. He grabs onto the ledge for a split second but immediately begins slipping. The impact of the landing causes CDR Sagez's chest to bounce off the rock. The extra weight of Kimmie makes it impossible for him to hold on to the ledge. As his grip slips, Henry manages to grab hold of his left arm just in time as their bodies sway. CDR Sagez winces in pain as his grip loosens a bit.

"Hold on tight!" Henry screams!

Amidst all of the panic and screaming, Kimmie's heart is racing. She is dizzy. She panics, wrapping her arms around his neck, cutting off his circulation.

"Help, help!" Henry shouts. Soldier-seven and soldier-eight rush over and desperately try to secure them. CDR Sagez's face is turning blue from Kimmie's inadvertent panicky stranglehold. Henry sees this and makes a decision. Once he believes that the others have secured the Commander, Henry reaches down, grabs Kimmie by the back of her shirt, and yanks her up in one massive thrust! This allows the others to easily pull CDR Sagez to safety as well! Thousands of deadly spiders look on angrily from the opposite platform.

Suddenly, there is a rumble in the cave. Their bodies start shaking with the

The Embittered of OZ

ground like an earthquake. The spiders flee immediately. Rocks and rubble fall from above the sinkhole. The rumbling gets louder and louder until the rope and several large pieces of rock fall from above and down into the sinkhole. The group looks around at one another in shock and awe, knowing that if this had occurred only moments earlier, they would have either died during the rope collapse or been stuck on the other side with no way across and deadly spiders to contend with.

Once Bitten, Twice Shy

Alpha and *Delta* teams make their way up the stairwell together. They travel up past the first three floors rather quickly. Trailing was CPL Ney, who had started feeling shortness of breath. He knew this was unusual because he was in superior shape. Then, he began getting dizzy and disoriented.

"I need to stop for a few seconds," CPL Ney announces. Everyone stops and looks at him. They were all perplexed a bit because he had been known to be in the best shape of all of them. He was the most physically superior of any soldier they had ever seen. CPL Ney took pride in proving his dominance in any physical contest they ever held.

"What's the problem?" General Gerns asks.

"I'm not sure," CPL Ney responds. He bends down and puts his hands on his knees again. He appears exhausted. They all gather around him. He stands up from a bent-over position. His eyes start watering excessively. "I don't know what's happening to me, but I feel very strange," CPL Ney proclaims.

"Did you get bit by one of those spiders?" CDR Jawa asks.

"I got bit on my ankle," CPL Ney admits.

"Oh, fuck!" CDR Jawa cries.

"What?" the general shouts.

"It's bad!" CDR Jawa says. CPL Ney starts drooling uncontrollably.

"What *da fug es gong* on?" he asks as he appears to develop aphasia and is unable to articulate his words.

"What the fuck is happening?" the

general asks in frustration. CDR Jawa whispers in the general's ear, "He only has minutes to live!" The general has been in many combat situations and is ready for almost anything, but even this is above his pay grade.

CPL Ney looks lost and confused. The others have no clue how to comfort him. They don't even know what is happening. They just look on in horror as it all happens so fast! CPL Ney begins having severe muscle spasms, twitching wildly. He is twitching so severely that he is obviously in extreme pain and significant discomfort, much like having a seizure. CPL Ney no longer is in control of his bodily functions. The crew is horrified! Death is one thing to them, but this type of suffering is considered sacrilegious for a soldier. CPL Ney falls to the ground. He lies in the fetal position shaking and foaming from the mouth irrepressibly.

"What the fuck is that smell?" Richard asks.

"He shit himself," CDR Jawa replies.

"Step aside," the general orders. He pulls out his pistol and aims it at CPL Ney's head. "You served us with honor! Now die an honorable death!" he declares, then pulls the trigger.

Boom!

Chapter 12 – Moment of Truth

The West Witch is meditating in her lair. She is conducting a ritual, standing in the middle of a pentagram drawn in white on the rocky ground. She knows this day has been prophesized for many years. Her downfall has been predicted to this very day. However, her pride would not allow her to believe she could be taken down. Moreover, her pride would not have her believe that she could be overcome by the likes of Suzanne, who, in the witch's eyes, is a nobody, an insignificant. She laughs and scoffs at anyone who even thought that Suzanne was her equal, let alone the one who was going to end her reign.

The Monvitas

Even though CPL Ney's gruesome death caused an immediate and severe drop in morale, the group outwardly shook off the mishap and remained focused on reuniting with Suzanne and the others.

Regardless, the memory of his death was still fresh in their minds. Only moments before, he was the viral, prideful, and snarky teammate they had come to love/hate. However, they witnessed his untimely demise, which saw his transference from a seemingly unstoppable force to essentially a person whose organs all collapsed at once within a half-hour's time. Still, they had to remain positive. This was not about them; it was about the future of their people and their families.

They followed the stairs up as far as they would go, hoping they would lead to the *West Witch's Lair*. They had no choice but to continue on this trajectory. They arrived at the fifth and final floor of the complex. They exited onto the fifth floor and entered combat mode to secure that level before deciding their next move. The soldiers split up, traveling in pairs. They went room to room, clearing each until they deemed the entire floor secure.

They walked down a long hallway that led to a lounge area with a couch and vending machines. They make a right and follow the hallway to the end to a locked door that reads, "Exit." There are also two other doors to the right of the exit door along that hallway labeled 501 and 502.

"This door is electronically locked!" Soldier-one announces.

"There is no power on," Richard says. "Shouldn't it open if the power is off?"

"Not at all," General Gerns replies. "If the lock is electronic and the power shuts down, the power must be restored in order to open it."

"So, what do we do?" Richard asks anxiously.

"We need to find a power source and turn it on to open this door," the general responds. "It is the only way we will get out of here." The general pauses for a moment.

"I think I spotted a control room a few meters back," CDR Jawa suggests.

"Before we do that, I want to secure the two rooms in this hallway," the general commands. He orders soldier-one, soldier-two, and *soldier-three* to check the room closest to the exit door (*room 502*) while he, Richard, *soldier-four*, and *soldier-five* secure the room next to it (*room 501*). The three soldiers enter room 502, and it's a mess. Two metal desks are lying on their sides, full of rust. Debris is scattered around the room. They look around and witness a mysteriously large, uneven hole in the corner of the wall, about six-feet high and four-feet wide. It seems as though something of considerable size had crashed through it. The hole connects to another room in the facility. They barely pay the other room any mind. There is also another hole in the ceiling in the corner near the hole in the wall.

"Secured," soldier-one announces, and they exit back into the hallway where the others are waiting.

"Did you find anything?" the general asks.

"No!" soldier-one responds. "Just a big hole in the wall and another in the ceiling in the corner of the room."

"Hmm," the general mouths, puzzled. "We found the same thing. Must be from some sort of structural deterioration. Lead the way, commander!"

CDR Jawa leads them back toward the cafeteria area. They make a left and then another left down a very short hallway that leads to a door on their left with the number 500 written on it, which is also electronically sealed. However, it appears to be a sliding door that requires a key card to open. Soldier-two removes his backpack and pulls out a crowbar. He uses it to try and pry the door open. It doesn't budge at first. However, he manages to pry it open just enough that several of the soldiers are able to fit their hands in and get a firm grip on the door. They pull and pull and finally dislodge the door from its holdings.

The room is filled with several large electronic servers that are lined up, creating three aisles in the room, and a small laptop computer at a desk that appears to run the whole system. They also see a hole in the wall behind the desk with the laptop on it similar in size and shape of the ones found in the other rooms that also leads to another room.

However, there still is no power. They search further but find no amicable solution.

"It's no use!" Richard announces. "We will never open that door! We are stuck here!"

"I think I found something!" soldier-three shouts as he searches a closet nearby. The crew rushes over to him. Lying there is a gas generator.

"Holy crap!" soldier-one shouts. "If this thing works, we should be able to open that damn door!" CDR Jawa switches the choke to the ready position. He then turns the control switch to the on position. He grabs the handle and pulls furiously on the recoil rope.

Vroom!

The engine roars for a second and then shuts off. The recoil rope draws back inside. CDR Jawa readies himself and pulls the recoil rope again with all his might.

Vroom, vroom!

The engine revs a second or two longer this time but shuts off again. He takes a deep breath and somehow pulls even harder this time.

Vroom, vroom, vroom, etc...

The engine turns on and maintains.

Some in the group cheer for the small victory.

"Soldier-four!" the general says. "How long will it take to get the system up and running?" Soldier-four is the electronics expert of the group.

"About ten minutes," he says as he sits with his back to the mysteriously large hole in the wall. "I just need to find and connect all the necessary wires, hack into the computer, and do a system override to open the door."

"Ok, great!" the general responds. "Get to it! We will maintain the perimeter!" They exit the room and leave soldier-four to work his magic. The rest of the group assembles in the lounge area. Soldier-one begins trying to infiltrate the candy machine. Soldier-two attempts to permeate the soda machine.

Two minutes or so go by. Soldier-two loses his patience, breaks the glass on the soda machine, and grabs a few drinks. Inspired by his cohort, soldier-one does the same with the candy machine.

"Who wants candy?" soldier-one asks.

"Oh, hell, yeah, Henry says. "Those look tasty!" He hands a package of candy to Henry. As the crew chows on expired junk food and flat soda, they hear several loud metallic thuds and rustling coming from one of the rooms near the exit. They all stop what they are doing. The sound was loud enough that they feared someone or something had entered that might be a threat to them.

"What the fuck was that?" Richard asks just above a whisper.

"Sounded like it came from one of the rooms down there," CDR Jawa responds, pointing down the hallway. The general holds his right arm up to his side, making an L shape with his arm and clenching his fist, a sign for them to keep quiet and hold their positions. They all freeze and remain silent for a few moments listening for any sounds. The general then waves his index finger back and forth toward the location of the sound. The troops walk cautiously toward the area in *staggered column formation*. Once they reach the two doors, the general holds his right arm in the freeze and quiet position again. They hear nothing.

They are positioned between rooms 501 and 502. Suddenly, they hear rustling in room 502. The general signals soldier-three to open the door. He approaches it slowly. He looks behind him to ensure that his mates are ready. They are! He grabs the handle and turns it slowly, trying not to make a sound. He then swings the door open quickly and stands back. They all aim their guns into the room along with their flashlights for a clearer view. Only soldier-three and soldier-five have a clear picture of the room as they both stand in the doorway. Soldier-three enters the room first. He waves his rifle and light around the room looking for any movement. Soldier-five follows close behind.

They hear a low rumbling, purring sound. Soldier-three anxiously moves his light and rifle toward the overturned desk nearby. Suddenly, a creature drops from the hole in the ceiling and lets out a terrifying screeching sound. Soldier-three quickly moves his rifle and light toward the beast, whose mouth is open wide and in mid-scream. He fires, hitting the creature in center mass, sending it to the floor where it remains writhing in pain. However, as he does so, a similar creature rushes him from behind the overturned desk. Soldier-five screams, "Oh shit, the *Monvitas*!"

The aggressive creatures are hairless, white-skinned humanoids that have a curved lower back and stand hunched over. Even with the hunch, they stand over seven feet tall. They are a semi-sapient species, so they display intelligence and even highly complex behaviors. They are tall, hairless humanoids with red eyes and very long, sharp teeth. Their teeth are unique as they have fifteen canine teeth on their top jaws as well as fifteen on their bottom jaws. This rare bread has thirty canine teeth, approximately 50mm wide (forty percent the width of the fangs of a male lion) and 13cm long (three centimeters longer than the fangs of the average fully grown male lion). It is important to note that lions only have four canine fangs. The *Monvitas* have thirty! One of them can kill a male lion in minutes if it can get a hold of one. They are as nimble as any animal species.

The nails protruding from their fingers are one inch thick and three inches long. They are razor-sharp and very viable weapons that rarely crack or break apart during massive impact. They also have nails on their feet about one inch long and one-inch thick, making them expert climbers. They have the ability to scale walls and other structures extremely fast. They cannot run at high speeds like the lion can. Nevertheless, they can reach top speeds of twelve mph.

Their skin appears white due to a lack of pigment from living deep in caves and only exiting during the night to feed. They're camouflaged into the rock, making them hard to spot, even in daylight. Their long nails help them quickly and easily scale surfaces that are impossible for humans to climb.

The *monvitas* leaps forward, covering a distance of twice its body length in a relatively short period of time. It lands on soldier-three with great force. Soldier-three was firing at the *monvitas* who dropped down from the hole in the ceiling. By the time he saw the creature that was upon him, it was too late. Soldier-three falls to the floor on his back. His rifle is dislodged during the attack. The *monvitas* sticks his claws into each shoulder during the takedown, pinning him to the ground as it bites deeply into his neck area. It clenches its teeth tightly into soldier-three's right trapezius muscle and pulls its head backward, tearing a large piece of the muscle away and into its mouth. Blood squirts out in every direction like a fountain. Soldier-three screams in agony as the *monvitas* casually chews on a large chunk of his flesh a few feet away.

Bang, bang, bang, bang!

The soldiers fire at the creature, sending him flying backward to his death. Soldier Three's trapezius muscle flies from its mouth as the creature squirms on the ground. Five more *monvitas* drop from the hole and quickly scatter around the room before the soldiers can get a shot off. Two of them promptly exit the room through the large hole in the wall, unbeknownst to the soldiers, who have taken cover. Soldier-three is still groaning faintly in agony while lying on his back. Blood is still pouring out from his right side. He soon passes out from the shock and pain. General Gerns orders an attack. Before his men can breach the room, three *monvitas* come rushing through the doorway. They fire!

Bang, bang, bang, bang!

Two of the *monvitas* are struck and are immediately taken out. Suddenly, soldier-five, who is standing at the rear near room 501, sees the door is open. As he turns his weapon to his right, one of the *monvitas* comes running out of room 501, charges him, and hits him with an open-fisted upper-cut to the right side of his ribs—sticking its claws into him and sending him to the ground. The *monvitas* jumps on top of him and bites into his cheek, cleanly ripping his mouth and jaw off his face just under his nose. The look of sheer panic in the soldier's eyes immediately following the attack is one of pure shock and terror as his eyes vacillate side to side and down, looking for the remanence of his jaw just before he blacks out for good.

Seeing the attack on soldier-five, the general orders a strategic move.

"Fall back to the cafeteria!" he screams. "Fall back now!" More and more *monvitas* jump down from the hole. Richard, CDR Jawa, the general, soldier-one, and soldier-two keep firing as they retreat to the cafeteria area. It was a brilliant play by the general, as he realized that they were outflanked and needed to protect their backside as well as use the aggression of the *monvitas* against them. More and more *monvitas* charged them from the hallway. The soldiers took cover behind any objects they could and made target practice out of the remaining quickly approaching *monvitas*.

As the last *monvitas* hits the ground, dead, they wait patiently for more to arrive. However, none do. After a minute or so, they hear a loud scream of agony!

"That's soldier-four!" soldier-one shouts. They all rush into the control room! They see a *monvitas*—who had snuck up from behind soldier-four through the large hole in the wall—chewing on the back of his head. The *monvitas* lets out a loud screeching sound when he sees them enter the room!

Bang, bang, bang, bang!

The *monvitas* is hit by several bullets and falls backward to his death. They take a few moments to secure the area and ensure no more creatures are roaming about before regrouping.

"What the fuck was that shit?" Richard asks.

"The *monvitas* are mythical creatures who no one has ever had proof of or have ever seen but have a rich history in this land," CDR Jawa explains.

"I didn't believe they really existed," says soldier-two.

"Yeah, well, they sure as hell do!" the general emphasizes. "And we have three dead soldiers to prove it!"

"How are we gonna get out of here now?" Richard asks anxiously.

"Let's try that hole where the monsters came from," the general suggests. "They must have some sort of elaborate tunnel system in there."

"Are you nuts?" Richard shouts. "You want us to go into the hole where they came from and likely run into more of them?"

"You have a better idea?" the general asks sarcastically. "We will move quietly and have the element of surprise on our side. There has got to be a way out through there. How else could these freaks have survived?"

"You know what they say?" Soldier-two says. "When the water reaches the upper levels, follow the rats."

"Who said that, exactly?" Richard asks.

"I don't know; somebody did!" Soldier-two responds.

"Yeah, could have been the West Witch for all you know!" Richard replies facetiously.

"The truth is the truth, no matter who it comes from!" CDR Jawa proclaims.

"Best to recognize truth then focus on who it comes from," the general declares. "Up we go!"

Trouble Ahead

Suzanne and her crew are exhausted. They climb up the vertical tunnel after the emotionally and physically draining Tarzan-swinging incident. They are climbing up the ladder of a tunnel the shape of a small round hole, approximately the size of a manhole, or thirty-four inches in diameter (*.86 millimeters*). It is a tight squeeze but a very manageable and unobstructed climb. A faint change in light can be seen a tenth of a mile above (*or 176 yards from bottom to top*). Soldiers eight, seven, and six are the top climbers, in that order. Suzanne is next, followed by Henry. Kimmie and CDR Sagez are holding up the rear. The soldiers all have their flashlights attached to their chests by Velcro, with the lights facing upward as they climb. This includes CDR Sagez, who illuminates the way for all above him.

"Slowly, slowly, one step at a time!" CDR Sagez orders. "Be mindful of each step!"

"I am claustrophobic!" Kimmie says anxiously as they reach twenty-five percent of the way. "I'm not gonna make it!" Kimmie stops. Her heartbeat is racing. She starts hyperventilating. Henry stops and looks down at Kimmie.

"You can do it!" Henry shouts optimistically. However, Kimmie grabs the metal bar with both hands, rests her head against it, and closes her eyes.

"I can't; I can't!" she utters. "I am lightheaded! I feel like I am going to pass out!"

"Keep going, Henry!" the CDR orders. "I got this!" The rest continue their climb. "Kimmie, listen closely! There is no rush. Let's take a timeout. Now, I want to ask you a question, okay?"

"Okay?" Kimmie responds in a crackly voice.

"Was if very hard to get to where you are now, physically?"

"Not really," Kimmie responds.

"Ok, good. Well, we are a quarter of the way to the top. Do me a favor, ok? Don't look up or down; just look straight ahead, at just the bar you are reaching for. I need to ask you some important questions." By now, Henry and the others are about ten yards above her. "Can you do that?"

"I can do that," she responds.

"What is your favorite food?"

"Huh?" she asks in confusion.

"Do you have a favorite food?" he reiterates.

"Uh, I don't know, pizza," she responds. "What the hell does that have to do with anything right now?!" she protests.

"Cause I am friggen starving," he replies. "I can't stop thinking about having a few slices myself. What is your favorite type of pizza? And can we just walk up slowly as we talk? Cause I need suggestions for dinner later."

"Yeah, sure," she says. Without thinking about her movements, she slowly begins climbing again. "I would have to say pepperoni."

"That's a good one. What about pineapple?"

"Pineapple?" Kimmie says angrily. "Who the hell eats pineapple on pizza? That is almost blasphemous."

"So, you are not a true pizza lover then?" the CDR asserts.

"What?" Kimmie says confrontationally. "I don't like pizza because I don't like pineapple on it? Do you like dog shit on your pizza?"

"Why would I like that on my pizza?" he asks.

"Well, I guess you don't like pizza then," she responds confidently. As her anger builds, so too does her adrenaline, which makes her unwittingly climb faster.

"Well, if you eat pizza, you really aren't getting much more than bread, sauce, and cheese," the CDR says. "The pepperoni doesn't provide enough protein, and you certainly are not getting any vegetable intake."

"First off," Kimmie says, irritated, "most nutritionists deem tomato a vegetable. Second, you asked me what my favorite food is, not what the most balanced meal is. Who the fuck is gonna say that their favorite food is broccoli? We eat that shit cause we should, not cause we want to. We invent new ways to cook and season it, so it doesn't taste like a fucking tree branch. And as far as pineapple on pizza, I had much more respect for you before this conversation, commander. I thought you were a man's man. But I guess it's actually pretty enlightening that you are in touch with your feminine side. I pegged you more as a bourbon on the rocks guy. But maybe you're more of a '*sex on the beech*' type guy?" Henry reaches down with his right hand.

"Come on, Kimmie, you can do it!" he shouts. Distracted by the conversation,

Kimmie didn't realize that she had climbed all the way to the top. Henry grabs hold of her arm and pulls her up successfully. CDR Sagez climbs up seconds later.

"I fucking hate pineapple on my God damned pizza!" he says firmly. Kimmie looks around in amazement. She has both a look of confusion and a smirk on her face. She is stunned and yet tickled that he tricked her. "I know your type. All I gotta do is contradict and provoke you, and your wrath will supersede your fear."

"Damn, you are good!" Kimmie responds, admitting defeat. "I'm a little offended that you played me like that, but I'm gonna let that go for now!"

The hallways appear to be much narrower at this higher altitude. The path leads in only one direction, forward. To their left is a *hole in the cave wall.*

"Which way?" Suzanne asks? Soldier-six looks into the hole.

"There is a hole here that leads down," she replies.

"I guess we have no choice but to follow the path in front of us," CDR Sagez states. They continue in the same formation, with the three soldiers leading the way and CDR Sagez holding up the rear. Little do they know, but they are on the bottom floor of the *six-level lair*.

They walk forward and around the corner to their right. They realize they are currently in *the tombs*. Jail cells line the area. Malnourished, sickly prisoners are everywhere and hard to look at. Some can barely move. Most appear emaciated. They seem to have all been left to suffer there till death. As the group walks by each cell, some prisoners start shouting for help.

"Quiet, quiet!" CDR Sagez shouts just above a whisper. One inmate is standing, resting against the bars, holding them with both hands. He is an older man with long grey hair and balding at the top of his head. He is very soft-spoken, yet, you can hear the urgency in his voice when he says to them, "Please help us! The guard over there had a heart attack or something a few minutes ago. He is over there on the floor. He has the keys on his belt." They look over and see the guard lying face down.

"We must help these people!" Suzanne avows.

"Once we kill the witch, these people will be free," CDR Sagez responds. "These people can barely walk. They will only slow us down."

"I don't care," Suzanne responds. "We must free them!" CDR Sagez carefully walks over to the unconscious guard. He flips the body onto its back and aims his gun at him, ready to fire with movement. However, the guard is clearly dead, and white foam is all over his mouth. CDR Sagez grabs the large keychain with several keys on it off the dead man's waist and hands it to Suzanne. Just as she puts it in her pocket, twelve armed guards appear and surround them. They are completely outnumbered. They drop their weapons upon command. Suddenly, the *Tin Soldier* walks past the guards with a slight limp. The look on his mechanical face is ominous enough to send shivers down their spines.

Henry and Kimmie look completely defeated. The color is flushed from both of their faces. They look hopeless. Suzanne, on the other hand, appears confident and unshaken. Henry looks at Suzanne, who is on his left. He is puzzled by her poised demeanor.

"This is it!" Henry says to her as if trying to wake her up from her delusional state.

"Not quite," Suzanne responds.

"What do you mean?" Henry whispers.

"Just trust me," Suzanne responds quietly. "I have a plan!"

"What plan?" Henry asks.

"Keep quiet back there!" one of the guards shouts.

"Just trust me!" Suzanne whispers. Henry looks at Kimmie, who is to his right. He gestures to her with a face of reassurance while slightly nodding his head up and down. This does not provide any comfort to Kimmie.

Chapter 13 – Backup has Arrived

General Gerns, CDR Jawa, soldier-one, soldier-two, and Richard have been climbing through the hole made by the *monvitas* for some time now. It splits in many directions, but they make it a point to move upward. They did not have the luxury of a ladder. Luckily, the narrow hole provided several natural hand grips along the way. As they reach the top and exit the hole, they notice a similar opening to their left, about the size of a manhole with a ladder leading down. They walk forward, the only direction that they can. They walk around a corner to the right and come upon *the tombs*. General Gerns quickly signals his men to halt as he sees Suzanne and her crew on their knees, surrounded by the West Witch's soldiers. They peek around the corner and see them being cuffed and led away.

"We must follow them, stay out of sight, and see where they take them," General Gerns orders. "We can formulate a plan at that time." The Tin Soldier and his men take Suzanne and her group through a door leading to a stairwell. General Gerns and his men follow covertly. Some prisoners call out for help to the general and his men. The general put his index finger to his mouth, ordering them to keep quiet as they follow Suzanne and her captors.

"We will be back for all of you shortly," the general announces. "I promise! Now, aid us in our attempt by remaining quiet." His demands are met by the prisoners. The general and crew enter the stairwell and stay a safe distance behind the captors. The general peeks up the middle of the staircase from time to time to see if they are still ascending. Luckily, the abductors' marching is loud enough that it makes it easy to follow them. The stepping of numerous soldiers echoed in the stairwell while the general and his crew tip-toed lightly, remaining two floors below them at all times.

While on the third-floor staircase, the general and his group hear a door slam above, and the footsteps cease. It becomes apparent that they had exited onto the sixth floor. They remain cautious and methodical when arriving at the sixth-floor doorway. Soldier-one slowly opens the door. Soldier-two quickly peeks his head in and looks down the hallway.

"Clear!" he whispers. They continue down the hallway carefully in search of their companions.

The Interrogation

Suzanne and her group are led down a long, winding cavern. They all have their hands in front of them, bound with electronic handcuffs. The technology of these cuffs is unknown to Sky People. Nothing like them has ever been seen on "earth." Their captors lead them into the West Witch's main room. Maura is sitting Indian-style in the middle of a pentagram. Her black eyeballs are rolled up into her skull. Only the whites of her eyes can be seen. Maura's concentration is broken once Suzanne and her group are led into the room. Her black eyeballs roll back into place. She looks at Suzanne with extreme disdain, with a blank, emotionless look on her face. Her eyes never move off of Suzanne.

Maura springs up awkwardly, unnaturally even, from the sides of her feet to somehow standing flat-footed. Maura slowly begins pacing side to side. Everyone in the group has a look of sheer terror on their faces as they are forced to their knees. They wait with bated breath for Maura to speak. The fact that she remains silent for a minute or so only fuels their anxiety. Seeing Maura up close, her pale crackling skin and zombie-like appearance only exacerbates the horror felt within. She is lanky, with a flat chest and a flat behind, looking almost gender-neutral. She stops and looks directly at Suzanne.

"My sister used to say, '*We all have a monster within; the only difference is the degree.*' Do you understand what that means?" Maura asks Suzanne.

"I believe what she meant is that we all are capable of the same atrocities; it just comes down to a person's commitment," Suzanne answers. Suzanne believes that the witch is being somewhat reasonable with her questioning, and she takes the bate.

She figures that she might be able to out-reason her or persuade her in some way. It was the only choice she believed she had. Either way, she needed to buy some time.

"Ah, commitment!" Maura replies, enticed by her answer. "Please explain more."

"If someone wants revenge and is consumed by it, they will stop at nothing to get it. They are committed to it. However, another person might not allow it to consume them, and accept what they cannot change and move on."

"Interesting," Maura replies. "And so, you believe the stronger person is the person who is capable of accepting it and moving on, I presume?"

"Correct," Suzanne replies.

"And why is that?" Maura asks.

"Because it takes a stronger person to turn the other cheek," Suzanne proclaims. Maura starts laughing uncontrollably. The laugh sounds very creepy. She looks at her guards as she laughs, but they remain stone-faced.

"Oh, what a gross mischaracterization of reality!" Maura says.

"How do you mean?" Suzanne asks boldly.

"You think it takes courage to turn the other cheek?" Maura says as she chuckles a bit lighter this time. "Have you ever seen your government turn the other cheek? Have you ever seen those in power turn the other cheek to those opposed? That is a lie sold to you by your oppressors and bought by you. Only the weak turn the other cheek. The courageous do not run; they fight! I heard someone once say, 'violence doesn't solve anything.' But the ones who say that are the same ones who have benefited from violence, even if the benefit is inadvertent. It solves everything. I bet where you come from, the leaders are in power solely because their ancestors exhibited extreme violence in order to have their bloodline remain in power! Over time, the simple threat of violence will suffice to remain in control. Only violence can change things, or at least the threat of violence from a stronger opposition." Maura sighs, puts her head down, and begins pacing back and forth again. "Today, I will teach you that violence can solve many things, if not everything! Clearly, the threat of violence did not deter you. However, I am betting that I am willing to take violence to a place you would not; hence, to a higher degree than you are capable. So, I must raise the stakes to show you how serious I am. How *committed* I am!" Maura motions to one of her guards and points to Soldier-six.

The guard walks over and grabs Soldier-six by her collar and pulls her up to a standing position. He walks her forward toward Maura, then pushes her roughly back to her knees.

"Where are the others that were with you?" the witch asks.

"What others?" soldier-six asks, looking confused.

"I will ask you one more time," the witch says calmly. "Where are the others who were with you earlier?"

"I don't know what you are talking about?!" soldier-six responds, then looks at CDR Sagez, who nods his head slightly forward, validating that soldier-six had done her duty honorably by not providing that information. Maura looks at the Tin Soldier, who then walks up to soldier-six from behind. It raises the ax above its head and, with one hostile swing, cuts her head clean off his body. Blood squirts out of her neck like a fountain. The severed head flies across the room, bouncing and skipping across the floor.

Thud, thud, thud...

It rolls right to up to Suzanne, bounces off her right knee, and comes to a stop inches away from her. A collective sigh fills the room. Soldier-seven and soldier-eight both gasp, groan, and turn away. Filled with grief, CDR Sagez lowers his head. Blood from her neck had splattered onto Suzanne's right thigh. The initial blow sent blood spatter around the room, spraying most of those who were on their knees. Soldier-six's body falls lifelessly to the ground.

Thud!

Kimmie starts gagging and panting heavily. Henry winces and begins breathing raggedly. Suzanne winces slightly but remains poised otherwise.

"Now, go and get that leg fixed," the witch commands the Tin Soldier, who will head to a private room within the cave where it will be tended to by small *android robots, known as maintenance robots (MRs)*, who will repair it. On its way out, it grabs soldier-six's head and lifeless body and drags her body away, leaving a fresh blood trail in its wake.

****

In another section of the witch's lair, the *Head Maiden*, who is in charge of all kitchen activities, paces the kitchen, ensuring everyone is hard at work and attending to their duties. Each of the seven female *cooks/hostesses* has a specific job. They are all wearing cloaks with hoods on as to not be individualized. They are preparing for a night feast to celebrate the retrieval of the East Witch's ring. The power that it wields by someone who can harness it is immense. However, the power it can wield in combination with another of the four rings changes the balance of power entirely in the West Witch's favor. She will be unstoppable with two of the four rings.

The Head Maiden introduces a new

female cook to the crew.

"Her name is *Misteen*, and she is filling in for *Magdulan*, who has apparently fallen ill and has not informed any of us again. Several hostesses begin chattering amongst themselves, skeptical of the newcomer. "Since she is new here, Misteen will be responsible for bringing the witch the poison for the execution ceremony. All of the other cooks let out a sigh of relief.

****

"Bring her to me!" the West Witch commands of one of her guards. He walks over to Suzanne and roughly pulls her up by her right arm. Suzanne grunts in pain as he grasps her and pulls her with no regard. He drags her a few feet closer to the witch and pushes her down at the witch's feet.

"I am not able to kill you, nor am I able to order your death while you are wearing my sister's ring. If you give me the ring now, I promise you a quick and painless death, and I will let your friends go in peace. I suggest we have a drink and further discuss my terms."

"I will not take off this ring until I am back home!" Suzanne says adamantly.

"Is that so?" the witch asks. Suzanne nods her head up and down confidently. Kimmie looks at Henry with a shocked look.

"I think she has gone crazy!" Kimmie whispers regarding Suzanne.

"Your other option is to watch your friends die a slow and painful death; then, you will be locked away permanently until you die on your own, at which time I will retrieve the ring from you. Death is the only thing that can break the covenant if you are unwilling to part with it."

"Can't you just let us go, and I will have a messenger deliver you the ring once we are safe?" Suzanne asks.

"And you think that you will get away with murdering my sister?" the witch asks.

"It was an accident, I swear!"

"Silence!" the witch screams loudly. The witch is now angry, and this is reflected in her new tone of voice. "You are in no position to negotiate." The witch turns and walks back to her cauldron that is boiling over with some sort of magic spell ingredients. She positions her head above it, closes her eyes, and takes a deep breath. She exhales, then lets out a sigh of satisfaction. "Bring the tall one to me!" she orders, speaking of Henry. Two guards grab Henry's arms from each side and drag him forward.

"Wait!" Suzanne shouts. "Ok, I will give you the ring!" Maura stops in her tracks. A look of bewilderment consumes her face for a second. "I will take that drink since it shall be my last," Suzanne announces. "And I have some terms of my own to negotiate."

Henry and Kimmie both look terrified and puzzled at the same time. They are flabbergasted by Suzanne's display of bravado. The guards return Henry to his original position after the witch flashes a hand gesture.

"What the hell is she doing?" Kimmie asks Henry.

"I don't' know," he responds. "But I think she has a plan."

"A plan?" Kimmie asks. "What, to get killed and get us killed so she can have a fucking drink?"

"Just be cool, Kimmie!"

The witch gestures again to the guard, who immediately retreats into the kitchen. Upon his arrival, the Head Maiden looks at the girls. "It's time!" she says anxiously. One of the hostesses hands the new cook two cups filled with liquid.

"The one in your right hand is filled with poison!" The Head Maiden firmly points out. "The one in your left hand has no poison in it. You must give the drink in your right hand to Maura and the one in your left to the traitor. Can you do that?"

"But the one in my right hand is poison," Misteen says. "Why would I give Maura the poison one?"

Just do as you are told!" the Head Maiden replies. Can you do that?"

"Of course," Misteen replies. "The one in my right is filled with poison. I will place it in front of Maura!"

"Remember, this is your right of passage and will make you one of us," the Head Maiden declares. "Once you put down the drinks, retreat to the corner of the room, keep your head down, and wait for the drinks to be finished. Then, retrieve the cups and head back here, understood?"

"Yes, not a problem," Misteen replies.

"Good!" The Head Maiden responds. "*Anafin* will accompany you to be sure the task is completed correctly."

"I really don't need a chaperone," Misteen replies.

"Oh, but you do!" the Head Maiden orders.

Misteen and Anafin enter the library. Misteen sees Suzanne sitting comfortably on the brown leather couch. Maura is pacing around slowly, perusing the bookshelves. Misteen walks toward Suzanne. Anafin is trying to peek around to get a good look at the cups in Misteen's hands, but Misteen's back is blocking her view. Misteen quickly switches the cups, putting the one in her right hand into her left and the one in her left hand into her right.

Misteen puts the drink in her right hand on the coffee table opposite Suzanne, where another brown leather couch rests. She puts the drink in her left hand in front of Suzanne, next to the electronic handcuffs that had been removed from Suzanne's wrists. Misteen nods her head at Suzanne and then gestures with her eyes toward the cup across from her. Suzanne nods her head in understanding.

"Thank you!" she replies.

Misteen retreats to the corner of the room and settles next to Annafin, who witnessed the transfer. Annafin nods in approval of Misteen's proper placement of the cups. They both put their heads down and remain motionless.

"Have you ever read the book, Moby Dick?" Maura asks as she reaches up to the fourth shelf and grabs the book.

"Yes. It was required reading in high school where I come from for many years," Suzanne explains.

"I came upon it after killing a few sky people," Maura mentions. "One of them had the book in their possession. It was very enlightening, to say the least."

"What did you make of it?" Suzanne asks. Maura is staring at the cover of the book.

"In the beginning, it appeared as though the whale was the evil one. However, as you read on, you realize that it is Captain Ahab's obsession with the whale that consumed him to the point that he was no longer rational. The whale was always just trying to escape capture."

"Emotional responses without proper consideration will ultimately lead to an irrational response," Suzanne replies.

"You are very wise," Maura says. "I was not expecting that."

"Why, thank you!" Suzanne replies.

"Let's have that drink and discuss this situation," Maura says. She slides the book back into place and takes a seat on the couch across from Suzanne. Maura grabs her cup and raises it. Suzanne does the same. They touch glasses. However, they are both reluctant to drink. Suzanne brings the drink to her mouth but stops just before taking a sip.

"What's the matter?" Maura asks. "You think I would poison you?"

"Something Like that!" Suzanne says. "I know you can't kill me, but if I kill myself, that absolves you, and you get the ring."

"How about we switch cups then, as a show of good faith?" Maura asks.

"Ok, fine," Suzanne replies. The two

exchange cups. "You first," Suzanne says. Maura obliges, downing the entire contents of the cup and slams it on the table. Suzanne looks at her own drink skeptically. After a few seconds, she chugs the drink. Annafin takes a step forward to retrieve the empties. Misteen puts her hand out, stopping her from doing so. Annafin is a bit stunned. However, she does not dare cause a scene in front of the witch. She figures she will deal with it later.

"You know, I have learned much from you, Sky People," Maura says. "And I must say, you might be the smartest I have ever encountered. I think I might actually regret killing you."

"You are still going to kill me?" Suzanne asks. "I thought we were negotiating?" Maura chuckles.

"You Sky People amuse me so. I might make some of your friends my pets. But you, my dear, you will be dead in less than five minutes. No offense, but if I were to let you live, it would show weakness on my part. You killed my sister; whether by accident or not, you must die. Plus, I actually enjoy watching people die an agonizing death."

"So, how are you going to kill me?" Suzanne asks.

"You killed yourself by switching drinks. I knew you would question the drink. So, I made sure that I was given the poisoned drink. That way, when I switched with you, you would never suspect that you were drinking poison." Maura can't help but chuckle at her own cunning.

"Interesting," Suzanne replies. "But what if my plan the whole time was to make sure that you drank the poison?"

"What do you mean?" Maura asks, exhibiting a look of worry on her decrepit face.

"What if the woman who served the drinks tipped me off as to which one was the poison?"

"Impossible!" Maura declares. "My servants are loyal! My spell over them is impenetrable!"

"True," Suzanne says confidently, "but what if someone infiltrated your loyal crew at my behest and tricked you and your crew?"

"Impossible," Maura giggles

uncomfortably. She looks around the room. She sees the two hooded women in the corner. "Both of you, come forward!" she commands. As her two servants slowly approach, Maura's stomach begins rumbling. She starts coughing lightly. She is having a hard time catching her breath. Maura starts dry heaving mildly. Her servants settle at the edge of the couch. Suzanne is smiling incessantly. "Who are you?" Maura asks.

"I am Annafin. I have been with you for several years, your majesty!"

"Yes, Annafin," Maura replies with comfort and a sigh of relief. "And you?" she asks of the other.

"I am," the woman pauses for a moment. Then, she hostilely removes her hood. "I am *Doria*, you piece of shit! And I am here to see you dead!" Maura is in shock and a bit confused! However, anger and immediate retribution take first priority.

"Guards!" Maura yells. However, her shout was interrupted by a blockage in her throat. "Guards!" she tries again. This call was even more subdued than the one before. Maura tries desperately to swallow. She grabs her throat with both hands. "Guards!" This shout attempt was just above a whisper. Each word she tries to utter becomes increasingly more difficult. Then, she starts coughing incessantly. She instinctually covers her mouth with her right hand. After a few moments of incessant coughing, she looks at her right hand and sees blood splatter. Anafin looks on in shock and remains frozen.

The witch's coughing increases, as does the amount of blood that shoots from her mouth. White foam starts to form around her lips. Within a few moments, the blood is blocking her airways. She begins choking and gasping for air that will not come. Doria looks down on her suffering with only contempt and disdain. Suzanne just sits back calmly. After several minutes of shock, Anafin runs out of the room to go and get help.

By now, Maura stands to her feet. She walks awkwardly toward the bookshelf and leans over. She is coughing up an enormous amount of blood.

"You were right about one thing!"

Doria says angrily. Maura has both hands on her own neck and falls to her knees. "You were right that if I crossed you, I wouldn't live to regret it! Well, I don't regret it at all!" The veins in Maura's neck start popping out as she struggles to breathe. White foam begins spewing out of her mouth and down her chin as her body starts twitching uncontrollably. She stands to her feet. Her body inadvertently shakes her back toward the couch she was sitting on earlier. Guards and cooks come running into the room and witness the treacherous demise of their leader. Within a few seconds, the West Witch takes her last breath. She falls forward. Her head slams onto the glass coffee table, shattering it into pieces.

The West Witch is dead!

****

Suzanne and Doria are speechless for a few moments as they stare at the West Witch's dead body. The guards and hostesses all look at each other as if they have no idea where they are or what is happening.

"I must go and free my sisters from the dungeon immediately!" Doria cries. Suzanne hands her the keys.

"Release all of the prisoners and meet us at the front entrance of the lair," Suzanne instructs. Doria nods her head and rushes off!

Suzanne returns to the witch's main room where the others are being held. To their surprise, the two guards holding them captive moments earlier are now willingly removing their electronic handcuffs.

"What the hell is going on?" Kimmie asks as her handcuffs are being removed from her wrists.

"She is dead!" Suzanne replies tranquilly.

"Who's dead?" Kimmie asks.

"The witch?" Henry asks.

"Yes, she is dead!" Suzanne reiterates. "Doria poisoned her.

"Who is Doria?" Kimmie asks.

"It's a long story," Suzanne responds. "But it is over now." Suzanne looks at the guard. "Collect the rest of the servants and meet us out front. You are all coming with us."

"Why are we taking them with us?" Kimmie asks in opposition.

"The witch is dead," Suzanne proclaims. "Her spell over them died with her!"

Chapter 14 – Return to Emerald City

Feast in the East

The witch's former soldiers led the festive march back to the Emerald City. Chants of "Su-zanne" repeated sporadically for the several hours it took them to enter the capital of Oz. Suzanne and her crew were led back in luxury, riding in horse-and-carriage, along with the general and the remaining soldiers that survived the ordeal. Three carriages in the middle of the former army of the witch, each pulled by two horses, carry the mission survivors. Suzanne, Henry, General Gerns, and soldier-eight are riding in the *first carriage*. Kimmie, Richard, CDR Sagez, and Soldier-seven are riding in *the second*. CDR Jawa, soldier-one, and soldier-2 are in *the third*.

Kimmie and Richard are sitting next to each other and are inseparable. Suzanne was happy, but most of her happiness was focused on getting home. Sure, she was ecstatic that they completed the mission of killing the West Witch and liberating the land. However, for them, it was all a means to the end of returning to their homeland. Kimmie, however, reveled in the praise she was receiving. She milked it with several boastful gestures to the crowd as they stopped periodically along the way to show their thanks. She played to the crowd perfectly, sometimes getting them even more fired up with her charisma.

"I'm so sorry that you lost all those men!" Suzanne laments.

"Me too!" General Gerns responds. "But they were happy to give their lives for such an outcome. And, even though they are not here to witness it, they are as much as a part of it as any of us."

"I agree!" says a choked-up Henry. "They are heroes and should always be remembered and celebrated as such!"

"I would have gladly died for this result!" the general states. "And, I gotta be honest," he says as directly as a straight shooter could say it, "I didn't think you'll had it in ya! I thought it was a death mission for us all. But ya proved me wrong. And, I am honored to have served beside you," he says as he looks at Suzanne. "You are indeed the chosen one, something I did not at all believe prior to this mission!" Suzanne turns and looks out the window of the carriage. The words *"chosen one"* seemed to have triggered her into deep introspection. Henry and the general continue chatting as Suzanne retreats into her mind. The chatter from them becomes unintelligible to her, and soon fades. She stares at the passing scenery while in deep thought. 'Was this truly my destiny?' she thought. 'Is this really happening?' She replays some of the recent, pivotal moments in her head as she gazed upon the countryside.

However, those thoughts were soon intercepted by memories of her family back home. Moreover, she visioned what they must be thinking of her disappearance and the agony they must be feeling. It broke her heart to think of her mother and father agonizing over her vanishing. She prayed that she would get to see them again soon. No matter how extreme the circumstances she had faced or was about to face, it was as if she had tunnel vision. There was ultimately only one thought repeating over and over in her head: get home to mom and dad! Nothing else really mattered or even seemed real or important. It was her one and only motivation from the start. Without that *hope* or driving force, as strong as she was, she may have just acquiesced to the West Witch's demands without question out of complete indifference and a lack of will to carry on.

Word of the West Witch's demise spread quickly. It preceded the group's arrival into the Emerald City. After several hours of traveling, the group is met at the outskirts of the Emerald City by just about everyone who lives there. More cheers roared as the group approached. This was literally the most momentous day in the history of Oz and would go down as such in every book to be written. The history of Oz will forever show this day as the before and after date. This was the first day of the new era in Oz.

As the group approached, the awaiting crowd wore anticipatory grins as they parted and made a path for the returning heroes to walk through leading straight to the castle doors.

"We should get out and walk the rest of the way," the general suggests. "If we don't show our face's they might charge the carriages."

"Damn, now I know what the *Beatles* felt like!" Henry mentions.

Suzanne and the rest of her group exited the carriage and walked the rest of the way. The crowd threw roses and other flowers at the group symbolizing their respect and admiration for them. Kimmie picked up a rose off the ground, held the stem between her teeth, and waved at the people as she walked by them, providing numerous bows along the way. As they reach the castle doors, Marlee is there to greet them. They stop, and the rowdy crowd settles down in anticipation of Marlee's impending announcement.

"Ladies and gentlemen!" Marlee shouts from atop a carriage. "Will you please help me welcome home the brave souls who have defeated the West Witch, Maura, and liberated Oz!" A sustained load cheer lasted for more than two minutes.

Thunderous applause from the crowd showed their appreciation. "In honor of our returning heroes, and of course in remembrance of the fallen, an honorary feast and celebration will be held tonight in the main banquet hall! Come one, come all! The crowd exclaims with extreme excitement as the honored heroes enter the castle.

Return to the Castle

Marlee leads the group inside to the enormous *Main Hallway* with the ceiling reaching a towering thirty feet in length. Barkley is there to greet them.

"So, you really did it, huh?" Barkley asks in amazement.

"She is dead as dog shit," Kimmie proclaims.

"I heard; I heard," Barkley says. "Do you have proof?" Suzanne extends her right hand toward him, fist clenched. She stretches it outward, turns her palm facing upward, and unclenches her fist. Resting in her palm is the ring of the West Witch. Barkley's eyes open wide in amazement. He immediately reaches out and grabs it. He pulls the ring close to his eyes and gazes at it with astonishment. He indeed authenticates that it is the West Witch's ring and most prized possession (one that she would have only parted with upon death).

"Well, well! I have to say, I was not expecting you to complete such a laborious task," he declares.

"It wasn't easy, and it wasn't fun!" Suzanne replies. "We lost several people during this mission."

"Yes, yes," he responds while staring at the ring. He breaks his gaze and looks up at Suzanne and the general, and his facial expression shifts to that of a serious nature. "Those who have given their lives for this cause will be remembered and celebrated for all time. Their families will be taken care of handsomely. They have saved so many with their actions. You all have!" he pauses for a moment and looks at the survivors, who are awaiting his response. "We will feast in honor of the fallen and in honor of you who have returned! You are forever heroes of Oz, and the Wizard will be oh so delighted to provide you with anything your heart's desire."

"We have already told you what we want," Suzanne says as she looks at Henry and Kimmie.

"Yes, yes," Barley says dismissively, "we have plenty of time to discuss that. But now, you should go wash up, rest, and prepare for the festivities."

Victory Celebration

Henry, Kimmie, and Suzanne are all dressed nicely for the celebration. The South Witch had magically conjured up clothing for them and had the clothing resting on their beds as they arrived at their rooms.

Music is being played by a DJ, and many people are dancing.

"I'm getting a strange feeling about this Barkley character," Suzanne mentions to the others.

"What do you mean?" Henry asks.

"I don't know," Suzanne replies. "Something is a little off with him. I don't trust him."

"Well, we did what the Wizard asked us to do," Kimmie responds. "Now we get to go home. But first, we drink!"

"Hey, no getting wasted like last time!" Henry asserts.

"Don't worry," Kimmie says. "Richard will look after me." Richard comes walking over at that moment. "Oh, speak of the devil. You look so handsome."

"Why, thank you, my dear. May I have this dance?"

"I thought you'd never ask," Kimmie says, jokingly, as she pushes her hair off her shoulders with her right hand. Richard nods at Suzanne and Henry, then leads Kimmie to the dance floor.

"We need to keep an eye on Barkley," Suzanne says. "I need to know more about this guy. The queen said the wizard is a sky person."

"That means he is from earth," Henry replies. "Wait a minute, we don't have wizards on earth!"

"Exactly!" Suzanne responds.

"Ok," Henry replies. "Let's split up and mingle, so we don't seem conspicuous."

Everyone at the gathering wants a chance to speak to the heroes. Everywhere Suzanne or Henry went, people were congratulating them. Some stopped them and wanted to hear first-hand accounts of their heroic journey. They mingled gracefully while still keeping an eye on Barkley, who was also making his rounds. Kimmie and Richard remained on the dance floor, oblivious to Suzanne and Henry's plans. The mayor of *Tiny Town* and others watched as Kimmie danced mockingly, amusingly to the music.

"Those Sky People are a bit strange, no?" he says, speaking to another dignitary to his right. The man shakes his head up and down while looking at Kimmie oddly. Barkley is chatting with several people and begins looking around suspiciously while doing so. Suddenly, he excuses himself and walks out of the *Ballroom* abruptly. Suzanne and Henry are on opposite sides of the room, both engaged in conversations of their own. Suzanne looks at Henry and nods her head in Barkley's direction. Henry looks up and sees Barkley leaving the room. They both excuse themselves and covertly rush after him. They meet at the Ballroom exit and enter the main hallway.

They quickly look right and see nothing. They look left and see Barkley's head descending down the stairwell. Suzanne puts her right index finger to her lips.

"Shhh!" she utters. They secretly follow Barkley down the stairs, doing their best to remain unheard and unseen. Barkley exits the staircase onto the basement level. This medium-sized hallway appears to be the hub that leads to all areas of the enormous basement. Suzanne and Henry do not know at this time that the castle's basement is a labyrinth with many secret rooms and one area not even showing up on the blueprints.

As Barkley exits the stairs, there is a door to his right, a door straight ahead, and a door to his left. Barkley makes a left and walks through that door. Suzanne and Henry peek out of the stairwell and see the door on the left closing slowly.

"This way!" Henry whispers. There is a small glass window on the door. Henry watches as Barkley walks down the hallway and into another room, then makes a right at the fork and exits through another door. Henry and Suzanne rush through the first door and hustle down the hallway to the next door to see where Barkley is headed. They peek through the small window on this door and see Barkley walking down a long hallway. He makes a left and is out of sight. They quickly follow.

As they come upon where he had left their sight, they notice that Barkley is standing at a metal door with a numbered security lock-pad just to the right. They peek around the corner and see Barkley punching in numbers. However, as he is doing so, they cannot see the numbers as Barkley is standing between their eyeline and the security pad. Several beeping sounds ring out in succession. Suddenly, Barkley drops something. It's the West Witch's ring! He bends down to pick it up, providing Suzanne and Henry with visual access to the numbers he had punched into the keypad screen: *3427256*. Barkley picks up the large ring, stands up straight, and hits enter on the keypad. The door slides open, and he enters. The door slides closed a second later.

"Did you get that?" Suzanne asks.

"Three, four, two, seven, two, five, six," Henry responds.

"I thought it was three, four, two, seven, two, SIX, FIVE," Suzanne contends.

"No, no!" Henry says adamantly. "It was FIVE, SIX. We need to get it right on the first try or it might alert security!"

"Ok, well, let's give it a try," Suzanne suggests.

They approach the metal door. Henry enters the number sequence: *3427256*. He looks at Suzanne.

"Are you sure we should be doing this?" he asks.

"Oh, I'm more than sure," Suzanne responds.

"How can you be more than sure?" Henry asks. Suzanne flashes a contemptuous look.

"Just press enter!" she barks.

"Ok, here goes nothing!" Henry pushes enter. The door slides open.

Hiss!

As soon as they enter, the door slides closed behind them.

Hiss!

They walk down a short hallway that leads to an enormous facility that is clearly a laboratory of sorts. The short hallway leads to an octagon-shaped facility with four large rooms protruding outside the octagon at the back end of the facility. It is soon evident to them that this is some sort of secret facility known to only those with the highest security clearance in Oz.

"What the fuck?" Henry blurts out. "We are definitely not supposed to be here!"

"Yeah, well, we are heroes, remember?" Suzanne says. She is not scared in the least. In fact, she believes that this facility holds the key to them getting home. Moreover, she believes that if she can figure out what Barkley is up to, she will have leverage over him. "Maybe the Wizard is here somewhere?!" she suggests.

The first quarter of the facility is slightly elevated. There is a wall waist-high on each side with chairs lining it for observation purposes. The walls run from right to left, with a beak in the middle of each, allowing for entrance into the heart of the facility. There are ten scientists visible in white lab coats from what they can see.

They soon locate Barkley, who is speaking to one of the scientists. He walks with the scientist toward them. Suzanne and Henry duck quickly behind the observation wall. As Barkley and the scientist approach, they start to hear their conversation.

"So, you don't think it is possible to send these *Sky People* home?" Barkley asks.

"The probability of them successfully reaching their homeland is about ten percent," the scientist proclaims. Suzanne's face turns red and fills with rage. She mouths something unintelligible to Henry and begins to stand up. Henry grabs Suzanne's arm and pulls her back down, urging Suzanne to remain calm and not make a move just yet.

"Well, ok," Barkley responds. "I will tell the Wizard that there is no chance of sending them home." Suzanne stands up in anger!

"No chance of sending us home?!" she yells. Barkley turns and is in shock to see Suzanne standing there. Henry rises as well, reluctantly. "The Wizard sent us on a death mission to save Oz, promising us he would send us home, and now there is no chance, you say?!"

"How did you get in here?" Barkley asks nervously. "You can't be in here!"

"I knew something was fishy about you!" Suzanne shouts. "Where is the Wizard? I want to speak to him immediately!"

Woh, woh, calm, calm down, let's, let's talk about this," Barkley responds tensely.

"Talk about it?" Suzanne responds frantically. "The only thing I want to talk about is explaining to the Wizard how you have misrepresented him and how you make promises that you can't keep to serve your own needs. I will tell everyone of this, and they will listen to me. I am a hero, remember?"

"Ok, ok," Barkley replies anxiously. "Let's go somewhere private and figure this out, ok? I want to help you!"

"He wants to help us!" Suzanne says sarcastically as she looks at Henry and scowls.

Behind the Curtain

Barkley nervously leads Suzanne and Henry toward the right back wing of the facility. There, they come upon a door that reads *"Chief Scientist."* They step inside the large office. There is a brown desk, several books on the many shelves, a brown leather couch, two padded chairs facing the desk, several unique ornaments carefully positioned throughout the room, and several degrees and certifications hanging on the wall, all with the name *"Dr. Winkie"* written on them.

"I understand you are upset right now," Barkley mentions, "but you are heroes in Oz. You can live out the rest of your lives being praised and revered here. The threats to you are gone! You will never get such recognition in your own home. You will live like kings and queens here for the rest of your days." Henry shrugs his shoulders as if he is considering the notion.

"I need to speak to the Wizard directly!" Suzanne asserts.

"That is not possible," Barkley

declares.

"So, you are telling me that we have almost given our lives for him and this place, and he doesn't have the decency to even meet with us?" Suzanne asks.

"The Wizard speaks through me and will not meet with anyone else."

"Oh, how convenient," Suzanne says sarcastically. "You wanna know what I think?" Suzanne says. "I think you are a fraud! I think that there is no Wizard! You are pretending that you are speaking on his behalf, but it is you who is running things!"

"How absurd," Barkley says with a nervous laugh.

"I think that I should raise this theory with the queen and see what she thinks," says Suzanne. "Maybe she can order an inquiry to find out what's really going on here. Come on, Henry. Let's go speak with the queen."

"Wait, wait!" Barkley shouts. "Ok, ok! There is no Wizard!"

"Excuse me?" Henry asks.

"There is no Wizard! I'm a fraud!"

"See, I knew it!" Suzanne says to Henry.

"Are you telling me that you have fooled us and these people all these years, saying that you are speaking on behalf of the Wizard, but the Wizard doesn't exist?" Henry asks.

"Yes, yes," Barkley replies shamefully.

"That is genius!" Henry responds. Suzanne gives Henry the evil eye.

"It is not genius!" Suzanne replies disdainfully, "He is a con artist!"

"Yeah, but you gotta admit, it's one of the greatest cons of all time!" Henry says. Barkley smiles at Henry and nods his head.

"Who the hell are you, exactly?" Suzanne asks. "And is your name really Barkley?"

"My real name is *Francis Friedman*. I was a magician in the traveling circus. My thing was making a surprise entrance in my hot air balloon. One day, when I was making my entrance, a fierce gust of wind overtook my balloon, and before I knew it, I found myself in Oz. The people here believed me to be the prophet that they had been waiting for, for many years. They called him the Wizard. The oracle explained to me that a great Wizard would fall from the sky in a floatation contraption and be the first of two prophets. She said the wizard would help bring balance, and would aid the second prophet in killing the east and west witches. So, I told everyone that I was his right-hand man, the only one he trusted, and he would not reveal himself to anyone but me. And they bought it hook-line-and-sinker."

"And how did you get the name Barkley?" Suzanne asks.

"I was a huge *Charles Barkley* fan back home, you know, the basketball player. It was a while ago. You probably don't remember him."

"Everyone knows him!" Henry asserts. "He is a very famous basketball analyst now!"

"Analyst?" Barkley says, confused. "He was hated by the establishment. He used to say he wasn't a role model. People freaked out!"

"Yeah, well, he is beloved now for his realness and honestly," Henry states.

"Well, go figure!" Barkley replies. "I'm sure a lot has changed since I've been here."

"You Have no idea!" Henry emphasizes.

"Can we get back on track here, guys?" Suzanne asks, annoyed. "What is going on in this secret lab of yours?"

"I put together a team of Oz's finest scientists to work night and day to try and figure out this phenomenon. How did we get here, and why do people from the U.S. continually find themselves here, among other areas of research? We have had hundreds of sky people mysteriously land here since I got here. I heard stories that I am not the first and that a sky person landed here years before me and has been working with the West Witch, but that is just speculation. What we have theorized is that there are wormholes in the sky that are responsible for leading our people here.

"Wormholes?" Suzanne asks in confusion. "What the hell is a wormhole?"

"It would be better explained by the chief scientist."

Barkley presses a button on the intercom sitting on the desk and speaks. "Send in *Dr. Winkie* immediately!" Seconds later, a man wearing a white lab coat enters the room. "Dr. Winkie, please explain the concept of wormholes to them."

"Well, to put it in layman's terms, a wormhole is a theory that two distant points in space or time are connected by a tunnel. Now, the length of this tunnel is said to be significantly shorter than the distance of the two points, making the wormhole a shortcut of sorts."

"So, you are saying that we somehow went through a wormhole to get here?" Henry asks.

"Yes, Dr. Winkie responds. "And all of the subjects, or *Sky People*, who have arrived in Oz have come from a place they call California."

"So, there is only one wormhole, and it is in California?" Suzanne asks.

"There are likely several wormholes in the universe," the doctor explains. "We have located at least two wormholes in Oz that we believe lead to California and that have led you and others here. Other wormholes may lead to other locations. But we do not have the data on their whereabouts. We believe we have located one wormhole in Emerald City and one in Tiny Town, but we have yet to find a suitable way to test our theory."

"Wait a minute," Henry says. "You are telling me we arrived here through some kind of space portal?"

"Exactly!" Barkley responds.

"But how were these portals formed?" Henry asks.

"That, we do not know," the doctor explains. "However, in our extensive analysis of the skies above Oz, along with the locations that the sky people have been found, we have identified two significant, unique sphere-like areas, one over *The Emerald City* and one over *Tiny Town*. After further observation and testing, we believe that both are spewing out matter and energy consistent with what we theorize would be a wormhole. Combine that with the fact that all of the sky people have fallen within a close radius of these spheres, and we can make an educated guess that is what we are dealing with."

"Ok, this is all well and good information," Suzanne states, "but how are we going to get home?"

"Well, we are not one-hundred-percent sure about that at this moment," Barkley replies. Suzanne's face turns red, and her eyes well up with liquid.

"What the hell do you mean?!" she shouts.

"Let me explain," Barkley says. "Follow me." Barkley leads them into the main laboratory area where most of the experiments are taking place. As they follow Barkley and Dr. Winkie, Henry looks to his right and notices an unbelievable sight, even for Oz.

"Is that, is that..." Henry points, struggling to put together the words. Suzanne turns and sees it as well.

"Holy shit!" she shouts, pointing to a severely damaged saucer-shaped machine approximately fifty feet wide and sixteen-feet high. "That's a UFO!"

"A what?" Barkley asks. Henry is still speechless and gawking at the aircraft.

"An unidentified flying object," Suzanne explains. "It is not from our planet but from another."

"Which one?" Barkley asks attentively.

"We have no idea!" Suzanne mentions. "Our government won't even confirm their existence."

"But we know by their technological advancements that they are highly sophisticated beings, much more than you and I," Henry declares.

"Really?" Dr. Winkie responds. "We will need to pick your brain a bit later on that."

"How do you know all this?" Barkley asks.

"I watch the *History Channel* a lot!" Henry replies. Barkley looks puzzled by Henry's response.

"Wait," Suzanne interrupts. "You didn't find any little green men in or near the thing, did you?"

"We know almost nothing about this device at the moment," Dr. Winkie responds. "The craft was absent of any creatures when we found it a week ago. We have just begun studying it."

"Oh, boy!" Henry exclaims. "Some people got roaches hiding in their house. You got aliens, man! This place is a trip!"

They continue forward until Barkley stops at an odd-looking bicycle with two sets of peddles, a large fan at the back of the bike, and some strange-looking plastic tarp that is folded behind the fan.

"Doctor, would you do the honors, please?" Barkley orders. Dr. Winkie explains to them that they have recently invented two flying bicycles, each with two seats, one behind the other. Behind the second seat is a two-wheeled lightweight trailer carrying a fan angled slightly toward the ground and away from the cyclists. Attached to the backside of the fan is a flexible wing pouch that expands as the air from the fan is pumped into it, allowing the craft to take flight and remain flying for up to three hours. There is also an electric starter that fires up the biofuel-powered 172cc motor. The bike can soar to altitudes of up to 4,000ft.

Suzanne is very cunning and intelligent. She realizes that Barkley is in a vulnerable situation. She makes a deal with him that if he can get them home, his secret will be safe. However, if the attempt fails, she vows to expose his secret. Barkley (*The Wizard*) loves Oz and his status there and has no intentions of leaving with them. Now, he is as much invested in the crew's return home as they are. To see them leave and never return means his secret is safe. Barkley agrees and adds that the experiment must be kept top secret from the occupants of Oz.

Chapter 15 – One Way Ticket

Ride or Die

The following day, Barley met with Suzanne, Henry, Kimmy, Richard, and three laboratory scientists just beyond the castle's front doors. In order to keep their experiment a secret, only those involved would be present at the time of takeoff. It was the break of dawn, early enough that most of the city would still be asleep, especially after such a wild event the night before.

The two bikes have already been loaded onto the large open flatbed carriage and are covered by two large brown tarps. Six *maintenance robots* are loading the flatbed with supplies needed for the trip.

There are three carriages in total. Along with the large flatbed, there are two smaller carriages (open) with seating along the sides of the structure. Suzanne, Henry, Kimmie, and Richard are seated in the carriage at the rear. Barkley and the three scientists are seated in the carriage just behind the one carrying the supplies. The supply carriage is manned by one of the queen's armed imperial droids (*comprised of Black metal armor*). It also carries two S50 worker robots (*silver metal S50 models*).

Each carriage is being pulled by two wooly-mammoth creatures known as *Lumens*. These creatures share similar characteristics with bulls. An adult Lumen stands as tall as ten feet and weighs as much as nine hundred pounds. They have incredibly shaggy, straight fur that is so omnipresent that it covers their four legs from being seen. Some say that they look as though they are floating when they walk because of this. These creatures walk as slow as humans, which is very slow for most four-legged animals.

They begin their journey by heading toward the back of the castle in the direction of the large mountain that stands not far from where they are located. Kimmie and Richard are not aware of the whole plan. They spent most of the prior evening drinking, dancing, and getting reacquainted. Suzanne and Henry gave them a briefing of the mission in the morning on their way to the front of the castle. Barkley announces that he will explain everything to them once they reach the top of the mountain. He wanted to make haste in order not to be seen. Kimmie's eyes are half-open. She is clearly hung over and tired from her shenanigans the night before.

"So, you're saying we need to peddle a bike that flies through a magic hole in the sky to get home?" Kimmie asks.

"It's a little more complex than that," Henry says, "but pretty much, yeah."

"I should have stayed in bed!" Kimmie says with a sigh and a grimace. "It's too early for this hocus pocus bullshit!"

The lumens pull furiously uphill as they reach the steep incline on the winding dirt path leading up to the mountaintop. After just under an hour, the group reaches the top of the mountain. The ground is level and grassy in the area where Barkley orders them to stop. The two *maintenance robots* and the *imperial droid* begin unloading the supply carriage.

Barkley gathers the sky people together and describes in detail what must be done for this operation to be successful. Henry takes the first seat on bike number one. Suzanne sits in the seat behind him. The trailing bike sees Kim in seat number one and Richard in the seat behind her.

"Remember," Barkley warns, "You will need to peddle with all your might to get the craft airborne. You must hit a speed of more than twenty mph to lift off."

"This is such a bad idea," Kimmie says as Barkley readies them for takeoff.

They begin peddling. It takes a few seconds to steady the bikes and pick up speed. They are angled down the mountain slope with the purpose of achieving maximum speed. They are soon moving very fast down the hill, reaching a speed of twenty-two mph. Just then, the *Tin Soldier* jumps out in front of the first bike. They swerve, somehow avoiding it. The second bike swerves also, but the Tin Soldier gets a piece of them. The intrusion slows them down a bit. It gives chase. The first bike lifts off the ground and is airborne. The Tin Soldier is gaining ground on the second bike. It swings its ax aiming for the fan. It just misses it and the metal trailer on the bike. Sparks fly as its metal blade collides with the metal bike frame. Kimmie screams in terror. The second bike lifts off shortly after. Kimmie turns to the Tin Soldier and says, mockingly, "Stick that axe up your ass you rusty bitch!" Richard laughs and then sighs, a mixture of relief and terror. Suzanne's bike is traveling 25mph and is climbing steadily.

Just then, the flying lion swoops in out of nowhere and collides fiercely with the second bike, sending Kim and Richard falling over the steep mountainside. They fall perilously, screaming the whole way down. They bounce off of the sharp rocks. The bike breaks into so many pieces it becomes unrecognizable. Their bodies are torn into piles of mush from the impact onto the sharp rocks below.

"Oh, no!" Suzanne screams. "We gotta go back!"

"They're gone, Suzanne!" Henry asserts. "If we go back, we will die too, and they would have died for nothing!" Tears stream down Suzanne's face as she scowls and peddles relentlessly. The lion turns his attention to them and gives chase. They can see the wormhole just ahead. The lion chases after them fiercely and quickly gains on their position. He can fly more than twice as fast as their bicycle can.

"He is gaining on us!" Suzanne shouts. "If we don't peddle faster, we are gonna be buzzard food!" Suzanne yells out. Henry digs in. His face turns red. He is peddling with all of his might. Sweat is dripping down his face. The lion roars as he gets within twenty yards of them and is closing fast. They are seconds away from reaching the wormhole. However, the lion is seconds away from reaching them. It's anyone's guess which will happen first.

The lion opens his mouth. His large, ominous teeth are ready to grab onto any part of the bike. Suddenly, bright lights of electricity start flashing all around them with deafening sounds of static crackling. It is so bright that they both close their eyes and can no longer see anything. They enter the front of the wormhole and disappear from the sky above Oz. Barkley and his crew look up in awe as they see them disappear.

Their jaws are dropped; their mouths are open wide. One of the scientists' cheers. The others follow suit. Even Barkley lets out a victorious shout while raising both hands.

"We did it!" he shouts. "We did it!"

No Place Like Home

She opens her eyes. She is groggy, to say the least. She slowly looks around the room. Everything is blurry.

"Suzanne!?" she hears someone shout. She sees the silhouette of a person's head a few feet from her. Her eyesight is too blurry to identify any persons or objects. Her mind feels like it is still rebooting.

"Mom!" the young girl yells as she springs up from her chair and exits the room. Suzanne raises her left arm and looks at it oddly. Her vision is slowly getting better. She notices a small tube sticking out of the crease in the middle of her arm. She begins breathing heavily, then takes shallow, deep breaths. She feels a sharp pain in her back. She groans and whimpers in pain and squirms in discomfort. But the pain soon wanes. Her curiosity supersedes anything she might be feeling physically. Her adrenaline is pumping. Within a few seconds, she realizes that she is lying in a hospital bed. She looks around the room and notices a flat-screen TV on the wall playing the local news.

"The weather today in California is expected to be sunny, high around seventy-five degrees," the weather woman reports. Suzanne realizes that she is home—well, back in California, that is. *'Was it all just a dream?'* she wonders. She tries to sit up. She feels a sudden rush of pain in several areas of her head and body.

"Where the hell am I," she says aloud, although struggling to articulate the words. She puts her right hand on her aching head. To her shock and surprise, her mother and father come rushing through the door; her sister Beverly is trailing close behind.

"Oh, my God, she's awake!" her mother shouts to her father. They rush over to the bed.

"Where am I?" she asks.

"You are at the *UCLA Resnick*

Neuropsychiatric Hospital," her mother replies.

"What happened?" Suzanne asks them.

"We were hoping you could tell us, honey?" her father says.

"They found you in a field just off campus," her mother explains. "The doctor said you encountered some kind of fall from a high place from the bruises on your body, and you have severe head trauma. You have been unresponsive for almost two days now. We were so worried!" Suzanne's mother pulls out her cell phone and sends a text to Suzanne's brother, explaining to him that she is awake.

"Mom!" Suzanne shouts. "Give me your cell phone for a minute, please." Suzanne grabs the phone and opens *Google.com.* She types in *"Kimiko Liang, Southern California."* Several articles pop up. They all say the same thing: *Kimmie has been missing for nearly two months.* She scrolls frantically, looking for a picture of her. She stops scrolling suddenly. Her eyes widen with fear and shock. It is the Kimmie she was with in Oz. Tears start flowing down her face.

"Is everything ok, dear?" her mother asks.

"Give me a minute," Suzanne replies.

She sees a link in one of the articles about Kimmie that leads to a *YouTube video*. The title is *"Missing Woman's Mother Pleads for Help."* She hits play. Kimmie's mother gives an impassioned cry for help. "Please, anyone out there with information about my daughter; I need your help finding her," the emotional mother says as tears flow from her eyes. The woman leans over to her husband, who pulls her into an embrace. "My Kimmie, she needs me! She was so full of life! Anyone who knew her would tell you that she, at some point, put a smile on their faces. Oh, please, Lord, please, this can't be happening!" Suzanne's eyes fill with tears as she listens to Kimmie's mother's cries for help, knowing the final outcome.

She heads back to *Google*.com. This time she types in, "*Lorenzo Rodriguez, Los Angeles, California*." Several identical names pop up, with one in Sacramento. She clicks on the image's link and begins scrolling through the pictures until she sees one that is familiar. It is indeed the man she had traveled with in Oz. She clicks on it, and it leads her to an article explaining that Lorenzo has been missing for more than a month. A picture of his mother crying is also in the report. His mother pleads for anyone with any information about her son's whereabouts to come forward.

Suzanne is beside herself with grief. She had only spent a short time with these people, but she had come to love them. Then, she remembers that she went through the wormhole with Henry. She turns to her mother. "Was anyone else found with me or near me?"

"No, dear, it was just you out there. Are you going to tell us what happened?"

"I'm not sure, Mother. I don't remember. Give me a second to collect my thoughts." Her mother turns to her father, "Oh no, she has amnesia. She must have brain trauma." Her mother starts weeping softly. She puts her head into her husband's chest. He embraces her. Suzanne searches frantically online for Henry. She finds his picture and bio on the UCLA basketball team's website. His email address is there. She hysterically starts typing an email to him. She is so anxious that she simply writes, "Henry, is that you?" She waits for a second. Then, she realizes that it's an email and that he may not have survived reentry, let alone be responding to her message anytime soon. She hands the phone back to her mother. "I need to get some rest," she says. "My head is killing me."

"Let's let her rest," her mother says to her father and sister.

"Ok, dear, we are going to go to the cafeteria and get some lunch," her father relays. Suddenly, there is a ding notification on the phone. Her mother looks at it.

"Did you email someone?" her mother asks. Suzanne sits up quickly, pulling some of the wires out of place. She reaches out.

"Give me!" she shouts. It is a reply from Henry. She opens it. It reads, *"Suzanne, is that you?????"*

"Turn this up," Suzanne's father commands, regarding the news on the TV. Suzanne's mother grabs the remote control and raises the volume. On the bottom of the screen, it reads, *"Flying Lion allegedly spotted by several in CA."*

"Authorities say that several people have reported seeing a *flying lion* in the skies over California this morning," the male newsman says with a smirk. "After 2020, I'd believe anything," the female newscaster says, and they both start laughing.

"What a bunch of kooks," Suzanne's father replies. "Flying lion," he scoffs mockingly. Suzanne's jaw drops, and her mouth opens wide with shock and terror. She raises her head and gestures toward the screen.

"Oh, shit, no!" she shouts. "No!" Suzanne screams, then, exhausted, her head hits the pillow, and she once again falls unconscious.

The End

"The Horrors of Willville" anthology series is on sale now!

Also, be sure to check out Will's classic horror novel *"Nomed Station."* You'll never look at a train ride the same way again!

Please visit:

https://willsavive.com/

Facebook:

https://www.facebook.com/WillSavive